SHRINKING RALPH PERFECT

For everyone at LWC
- where would I be without you?

Acknowledgements:
Part of the inspiration for this book came from a visit
to Tim Hunkin's arcade machines on Southwold Pier.
Anyone who'd like to try out *The Frisker* can do so there.

Thanks to Penny and Michelle for the title!
And a special thanks to Holly - ace reader and cereal stargirl...

ORCHARD BOOKS
96 Leonard Street
London EC2A 4XD
Orchard Books Australia
32/45-51 Huntley Street, Alexandria, NSW 2015
ISBN 1 84362 660 8
First published in Great Britain in 2005
A paperback original
Text © Chris d'Lacey 2005
The right of Chris d'Lacey to be identified as the author of
this work has been asserted by him in accordance with
the Copyright, Designs and Patents Act, 1988.
A CIP catalogue record for this book is available from the
British Library.
1 3 5 7 9 10 8 6 4 2
Printed in Great Britain

SHRINKING RALPH PERFECT

Chris d'Lacey

ORCHARD BOOKS

Prologue

Imagine something horrible happened.

Imagine you heard a story so appalling your ears turned to ice and they dropped off your head.

Freeze. Freeze. *Clinkle*. *Clinkle*.

Ears. Imagine it.

Clinkle.

Crack.

And if this tale was so fearfully grisly (*earfully* grisly, I suppose you could say), just think what other calamities might happen – like your toes might curl to the size of pebbles. Imagine *that*, pebbles in the ends of your shoes. Walking around on shingle.

For *ever*.

What sort of story could do a thing like that?

This sort of story. It could.

Oh yes.

What's in it then, you wonder? Boggle-eyed monsters from a far-off planet? Blood-swilling vampires from another time? Ghouls and goblins? Wizards and witches?

No, none of that. What's so frightening about this

story is how ordinary it seems. Because *ordinary* things can happen to anyone. Me and you.

But especially you.

Take what happens at the start, for instance. Like our hero, Ralph, you're sprawled out on the front room carpet, reading a really good book about dragons, when you hear a gentle tapping at the door. You run to answer, but you'll soon wish you hadn't.

There's something awful behind this door. Something that's going to change your life. But you open the door, anyway. Why wouldn't you? Someone's knocking.

And look what's standing on your step...

That's right. A sweet-smelling, slightly deaf, little old lady.

Now is that gruesome or what?

Bad News

'Hello, Mrs Birdlees,' Ralph said kindly. 'Would you like to come in? Mum's baking a cake.' He held the door open and waited for the frail old lady to enter. She looked like a peg on an empty washing line – rickety, lonely, blown about by the breeze.

'Thank you, Ralph,' Mrs Birdlees sniffed. Ralph smiled. Mrs Birdlees often sniffed. She was always reaching for the lavender-scented hanky stuffed into the sleeve of her tight-knit cardigans; always blowing away a cold, she was. But not today, Ralph noticed, as the hanky came out. Today his next-door neighbour was wiping a speck of a tear from her eyes.

'Is everything all right?' Ralph enquired softly, touching Mrs Birdlees once on the arm.

Mrs Birdlees sniffed again. 'Oh Ralphy,' she croaked, giving him a hug (many years ago, Mrs Birdlees had used to babysit him), 'I'll miss you so much. My sweet, sweet child. Why can't the other boys be like you?'

And just as she said that, just as the frail old dear closed her mouth, there was a shout in the street and a gang of boys shot past on their bikes. Whoosh. Like a flock of angry sparrows. Bumping up the kerbs, banging on the roofs of all the parked cars. *O-lé! Olé! Olé! Olé!* they were singing. A popular football chant.

Mrs Birdlees quivered. Her small face paled with fright. She patted Ralph's cheek and hurried down the hall.

Ralph closed his hand into an angry fist. The gang, Kyle Salter's gang, was already skidding into Hollyhead Crescent. With any luck they'd stay there. Out of harm's way.

Ralph gulped hard and closed the door.

Tight.

'Who is it, Ralph?' his mother was shouting. She was bending down, pulling a cake from the oven. A smell of warm ginger crept through the house.

'It's only me,' Mrs Birdlees twittered, in a voice as tiny as sesame seeds.

Penelope 'Penny' Perfect greeted her warmly. 'Good timing, Annie.' She held up the cake for Mrs Birdlees to inspect.

'Wonderful, as always,' the old lady said.

And on that note, she started to sob.

'Oh, Annie. What on earth's the matter?' Penny glanced at Ralph who just shrugged his shoulders. He was still trying to work out why Mrs Birdlees had cried in the hall. And why had she said, 'I'll miss you so much?'

'Kettle,' his mother instructed quietly. She quickly turned the ginger cake onto a cooling rack. She took off her oven gloves and folded her pinny, then guided their neighbour onto a stool at the breakfast bar.

'Oh dear, this is dreadful,' Mrs Birdlees wept, gripping tight to Penny's hand. 'I've been turning it over and over for months. It's been awful, you know. A horrible decision. I hope you understand. It was the only thing to do. If you've any sense, my dear, you'll follow my example.'

Mrs Perfect swept her fringe to one side and sat down on one of the bar stools herself. 'Annie, I don't understand. Do what? What is it you've decided?'

'To sell, my dear. To sell.'

Penny drew a shocked breath. 'You don't mean the house?'

Mrs Birdlees nodded.

'Oh Annie, you can't. You can't move away from Number 9. You've lived in the Crescent since you were a tot. You're our backbone. Our life support. What's brought this on? The hoovering or something? If you're having trouble getting up the stairs with your leg, Ralph and I will help out. Won't we, Ralph?'

'Erm, yeah,' said Ralph, dropping a couple of tea bags into the pot. Normally he approved of his mother's good-natured sentiments, but he wasn't too thrilled at the prospect of hoovering. He had to tidy his room once a week as it was. So he was quite relieved at first when Mrs Birdlees said: 'It's not the cleaning, my dear. I'm as sprightly as I ever was about the old place. It's not that. It's these...' She looked over her shoulder, back down the hall. 'It's these *boys*.'

A teaspoon clattered across the breakfast room floor.

'Ralph,' his mother tutted.

Ralph mumbled an apology. His hand was shaking as he picked the spoon up.

'Oh, Ann-ie,' his mother sighed. 'You mustn't let these silly incidents upset you. Boys of that age, they—'

'Girls as well,' Ralph quickly put in. There was a girl in Kyle Salter's gang.

'Make the tea,' his mother said trimly, and turning back to Mrs Birdlees she continued: 'I know that things have been rowdy lately. The children have reached that age, I suppose. It is annoying, I agree. Windows being broken, dented cars.'

'Mr Cooper had a gnome in his pond,' said Ralph.

His mother warned him off with an icy frown. 'I'm sure it's just a phase they're going through, Annie. It happens everywhere. You mustn't let them drive you out of your home.'

Mrs Birdlees interlocked her fingers and brought her bony hands up to her chin. 'But my dear, it isn't the rowdiness,' she said. 'I can cope with the shouting and the crisp packets stuffed through the garden hedge. It's not that at all. It's the other things they do. The evil things. Do you know what I found in my letterbox this morning?'

Not another gnome, Ralph was thinking.

Penny shook her head.

'Five dead bees.'

'Oh! Now that *isn't* nice. That really is disgusting. You should go to the police.'

'No,' said Annie, 'I should just go; pack up and leave. I have an estate agent coming round tomorrow. As soon as I find a suitable buyer, I'm away to live with my sister in Totnes. I'm sorry, my dear. For you, too, Ralph.'

Ralph nodded. On the breakfast bar in front of him, the automatic kettle blew a long head of steam and switched itself off. Ralph poured the boiling water into the pot. He didn't know it then, but it was the last time he would ever make tea for himself, his mother and old Annie Birdlees.

The End of an Era

Ants were Ralph Perfect's favourite animals. It seemed odd to call anything that small an animal. But Ralph had noticed that people, particularly old people, always shrivelled if you used the word 'insect' to describe an ant. 'Insects?' they would say, twitching their noses and scratching their arms. 'The only good insect is a dead insect, boy.' Ralph always shut up at that point. In his opinion, nearly every grown-up he had ever met was ready to do harm to tiny things. He hated that.

And he did like ants.

For one thing, they were just so fascinating to watch. It was the way they ran, whizzing about in dizzy little lines, up and over and round any object. Ants swarm, it said in one of Ralph's books, like a mini tidal wave. But Ralph knew ants were cleverer than that. They weren't really like a wave. They didn't just obey the pull of the moon. Ants went where they chose. Ants talked to one another. Not in the same way that people talked. The patterns they made meant things to other ants. It was a sign language, sort of. Like sending smoke signals or waving flags. Ants talked by their movements. They talked silently and fast. You had to *watch* them to hear them.

And Ralph watched them a lot.

The day things began to happen next door, he was lying on the patio, propped up on his elbows, studying a colony of worker ants as they swarmed round the water-butt at the side of the shed. Some ants were carrying dead ants about. They were hauling them over mountainous obstacles (twigs and leaves: mountains to them), before dragging them down through a crack in the paving slabs under the shed. They were going to the nest: dark and buzzing, tumbling with life. Ralph wondered what happened to the dead ants down there. Were they food for the other workers, perhaps? Maybe ants, like people, carried their dead to a special place to give them a decent sending-off. That made him think about old Annie Birdlees. Annie, moving to a different nest.

It was then he heard the voices in the garden next door.

His mother, who had popped out to throw some bread to the birds, heard the voices too. She looked at Ralph and put a finger to her lips. She beckoned him to join her at the garden wall. Together they stood, scouting through the holes of a honeysuckled trellis, spying on events in Annie's garden.

Mrs Birdlees was there, in a pair of bunny slippers and a cream-coloured cardigan. She was standing on one of the round stepping stones that curled in an 'S' down her long, narrow lawn. Her arms were folded like safety pins. She was shivering, despite the sun being out.

By her side was a smartly-dressed young man. In his hands he held a clipboard and a round tape measure. He was hopping about like a Morris dancer, cupping one hand above his caterpillar eyebrows and peering at the gutters of Annie's house.

'Oh yes,' he kept saying with solid enthusiasm. 'V. des. res., Mrs Birdley. Oh yes.'

'Bird*lees*,' the bemused old lady corrected him. 'What do you think, Mr Tattle, will it sell?'

'Sell?' Mr Tattle rattled, as if alarm clocks were going off in his ears. 'Oh yes, Mrs Bumblebees. Oh definitely, yes.' He took a small pencil from behind one ear and made a few ticks on the papers on his board. 'Period piece. Should do a bucket. Props. in this area, highly sought after. No FGCH or NDPC, but the spac. pat. makes up for it somewhat, doesn't it? It's a spangler, no swizz. Ninety K at least. An absolute lollipop.'

Ralph looked sideways at his mother.

'He's the estate agent,' she whispered.

'Why is he talking funny like that?'

'Like what?'

'Like he never eats anything but alphabetti spaghetti?'

Penny smiled. 'They just do. It's a sort of code. Mr Tattle was telling Annie that she doesn't have full gas central heating or a new damp proof course, but the spacious patio would probably make up for it.'

Ralph nodded, beginning to understand. FGCH – full gas central heating. But why had the estate agent called the house a lollipop?

'That's his way of saying the property is worth a lot of money. Sounds like they're going to put it on the market for ninety thousand pounds. Imagine that.'

Ralph tried. Ninety thousand pounds? Who in the world had that sort of money? He'd known his mother haggle about paying ninety pence for a bunch of bananas.

'Delightful garden.' Mr Tattle's voice floated over the wall again. 'Oodles of room for dev., Mrs Birdseed. Turn this place into a palace, you could.'

'Oh, I don't think so,' Mrs Birdlees said. 'What about the neighbours?'

'Good point,' said Mr Tattle, turning sharply. Ralph and his mother ducked under the trellis. 'Any probs. with nebs? The buyer could ask.'

There was a slight pause. Ralph thought he could hear Annie's hanky coming out. 'Mrs Perfect and her son are the best neighbours anyone could wish for. If I had the opportunity or the means, Mr Tattle, I'd take them with me when I go to Totnes.'

'V. commendable, Mrs Bindweed,' he said. 'Good rels. with nebs. Could make a diff. at the end of the day. Well, that seems about it. One or two 'p's and 'q's to settle, 'i's to dot, that sort of thing. Should have a board round first thing p.m. Okey-dokey. Must look sharp. People to see. Houses to sell. TTFN. Many thanks for using Tittle, Tattle and Parrot.'

Mr Tattle was true to his word. Shortly after two o'clock that same afternoon, a sign was hammered up outside Annie Birdlees' house.

FOR SALE, it announced, in gloomy green capitals.

Penny Perfect watched it happen. She stood in the bay of Number 11, eyes like a teddy bear: wistful, unmoving. When Ralph heard the banging and came rushing to join her, she slipped an arm round his shoulder and hugged him close.

'The end of an era, Ralphy,' she said.

Ralph nodded. Annie was really going. A pang of finality stabbed at his chest.

'Who do you think will buy the house, Mum?'

'Who knows?' his mother shrugged. She watched the man who had erected the sign throw his tools into a car and drive away. 'Someone nice, I hope. Someone friendly. Someone quiet.' She kissed Ralph softly on the top of his head and glided silently away from the window.

Ralph stayed in the bay for a long time after that. He took an elastic band from his pocket and twiddled it aimlessly around his fingers. His mind was a blur of change and worry. Old Annie, going. Annie, who had been as constant in his life as the sun in the sky, no longer coming out for her milk in the morning or sweeping the autumn leaves from her path. Instead, there would be an empty space. All thanks to the Salter gang.

Anger rose inside him, then. Anger and fear. Ralph hated himself for his dread of Kyle Salter. The bully was like a dark stain that never washed out. In a bid to push him far to the back of his mind, Ralph engaged in a game. A word-making game. He was clever and good with words. One of his favourite challenges was trying to make as many different words as he could from a single long one. He played it now with the letters: F O R   S A L E.

He was doing very well. He'd found 'foal' and 'safe' and 'leaf' and 'laser' ('for' and 'sale' didn't count, of course) and was trying to increase his overall tally by searching for the easier, three-letter words, when a loud popping noise broke his concentration. His gaze flicked briefly from the sign to the street. A grubby white van, pothering fumes from a rattling exhaust, roared past Annie's house and on up Midfield Crescent. Ralph thought nothing of it. Cars were cars: they passed by every day. He turned back to FOR SALE and had just spotted the word 'oaf', when he heard the sound of slowly-turning wheels and saw the strange, white van reversing up the Crescent. It backfired once and emerged through a parachute of blue-black smoke.

It stopped outside Annie Birdlees' home.

The van door opened on the driver's side. A tall, skinny man with hair as lank as seaweed got out. He leant one arm on the roof of the van, put a lit cigarette between his lips and squinted hard at Annie's house. He'd been like that for barely ten seconds when Kyle Salter screwed up on his bike.

'Giz a smoke, mister.'

The weedy-looking man didn't even sniff.

'Oi! Giz a smoke,' Kyle Salter tried again.

This time, the smoker's right arm moved. He lifted

the reddened butt from his mouth, twiddled it once and flicked it away. It bounced off Kyle Salter's chest. Kyle reeled back. His mountain bike reared. He flapped at his T-shirt as if he were beating off a wasp. Then his right foot slipped off the edge of the kerb and the front wheel of the mountain bike twisted away. Boy, plus bike, came crashing to the ground.

Ralph, in the bay window, had his nose pressed almost flat to the glass. He could hardly believe what he was seeing outside.

'You'll wish you hadn't done that,' Salter spat. He yanked the bike up, kicked the van and pedalled off.

That started a dog on the passenger seat yapping. All this time, the stranger hadn't moved. He hadn't said a word. He hadn't *looked* at Kyle Salter. Now, in a snarling, sandpaper voice he spoke to the dog, 'Git down, Knocker.'

Then he slid into the van again, slammed the door shut and roared away up Midfield Crescent.

A Buyer for the House

'What's got you in such a flap?' asked Mrs Perfect as she moved along the washing line, pegging up a pair of *Thunderbirds* boxer shorts. It made Ralph cringe to see his 'designer' underwear out on show. Honestly, the things his mother bought him for Christmas.

'There was this man,' he said, dragging his sleeve across his forehead. He was sweating slightly after rushing through the house.

'What man?' said his mother. 'Bring that basket over here, will you?' A green plastic linen basket half full of washed clothes was sitting on the stone mushroom by the small garden pond. Ralph went and fetched it.

'This *man*,' he repeated, holding the basket while his mum took out the clothes. 'He was tall and thin. He had a face like a gravestone.'

'No one's got a face like a gravestone, Ralph. Unless he had 'In Loving Memory' tattooed on his forehead. Where was he, Mr Cemetery-Face?'

'Out the front, looking at Annie's house.'

Penny took a peg from between her teeth. 'Oh? What

sort of looking?'

'I dunno. Just…looking.'

'Like what? Like a burglar? Was he snooping around?'

Ralph lifted his shoulders. 'No, he just looked. He knocked Kyle Salter off his bike.'

Mrs Perfect frowned. 'With a *look?*' she said.

Ralph sighed. Sometimes his mother was absolutely hopeless. He explained what had happened about the cigarette, the van, the yapping dog; everything.

His mother gave a slightly disapproving 'hmm'. 'He'll come to no good, Kyle Salter,' she predicted. 'What kind of van? Was there writing on it?'

Now he came to think of it, Ralph remembered there was. He'd seen a sign in black lettering along its side: IT WON'T WILT OR TILT IF IT'S BUILT BY BILT!

That was how it went.

'Built by Built?' his mother said.

Ralph explained the difference in the spelling.

'Ah, Mr Bilt the builder; bit like Mr Wedhem the vicar.'

'Yes, Mum,' Ralph said, hiding a groan. He watched a cabbage white butterfly dot about the garden. It landed on a vine of ivy leaves. 'Do you think he wants to buy it?'

Penny shook her head. 'The sign's only been up two minutes. She's probably asked him to do some repairs. People often do when they're selling up.'

Now it was Ralph's turn to give a little 'hmm'. A knot of nervous tension grew in his stomach. If the builder turned up again, things could get lively.

Kyle Salter wasn't the type to call off a threat.

Half an hour passed. Ralph mooched about. He read another chapter of his dragon book, then went out to post a letter for his mum. On Pear Tree Road he had to hide in the doorway of Frosts the Fishmongers when Jemima Culvery and Daniel Parkin (Jem and Dazza) came hoofing down the pavement playing kick-can, kick-banana skin, kick-anything they liked. They'd kick-Ralph, too, if he got in their way. The Salter gang. Everywhere. Like flies. A plague.

On his way back, he saw the white van again. It was pointing down the Crescent, parked on the opposite side of the road, this time. The brooding figure of Mr Bilt was standing just inside Annie's gateway, peering up at the front of the house.

To Ralph's mind, he didn't look like a builder at all. He was dressed in a shabby pin-striped suit that made him seem even thinner than before. The seaweed hair had been combed straight back and the worst of the straggles hooked back around his ears. He had a pointed chin and snake-like eyes. A cigarette was dripping off his lip. In one hand he was clutching a small brown box, which he held to his hip like a man of God might tote a Bible. In the other was a trilby hat. He was spinning it neatly around one finger.

'Hello.'

The hat ceased spinning and a dog began to growl. Ralph stopped in his tracks. He hadn't seen the dog and still couldn't. It was hidden behind the waist-high party wall between the two houses. He told himself it wasn't polite to peek over the wall and take a look. Secretly, he was slightly afraid of dogs.

'Git down, Knocker,' the man said idly. The cigarette leapt like the needle of a compass. The dog stopped yapping. The trilby switched hands. The visitor plucked the cigarette from his mouth and ground it flat underneath his heel. 'Well now, what have we here?' He looked Ralph up and down with the same sort of intensity he'd been giving to the house. It made Ralph shudder, but he wasn't afraid. He was on home territory. His mum was just a bell push away. He decided to make an effort.

'I'm Ralph; I live here,' he said. He pointed at the

Number 11 on the carved wooden plaque his mum had bought on holiday in Devon.

'Oh, do you?' said the man, raising phlegm from deep within his chest. 'Well, I'm Jack Bilt, and I'm going to live *here*.' He smirked and pointed at Annie's house.

Jack? Ralph thought. He knew a nursery rhyme about the house that Jack built. But he didn't dare mention it. 'Pleased to meet you,' he said, though he wasn't at all. He held out his hand for Jack Bilt to shake.

The visitor glanced at the pale pink offering on the end of the pale pink arm. 'Piano fingers,' he grunted. 'Washing-up hands. What they need is a screwdriver blister and a nice few splinters from a piece of two-by-four. Not much fizzing use, at all. Hardly been out of the *packet*, have those.'

Ralph withdrew his hand and buried it deep inside the pocket of his jeans. It wasn't the first time he'd been taunted about his physical appearance. There was the incident with Kyle Salter in the mats cupboard at the back of the school gym. But he didn't want to think about that.

'You're a builder, aren't you?' he said, straight up.

'And you're a clever dick,' the builder replied.

Ralph frowned, wondering what he'd done to offend the visitor. 'I can read,' he sniffed, looking across at the words on the van. For the first time he noticed another piece of writing, in brackets under the original sign.

The whole thing read: IT WON'T WILT OR TILT IF IT'S BUILT BY BILT! (AND HIS MINIONES)

'I can spell, too,' Ralph continued.

The visitor eyed him sharply.

'I don't think there's an "e" in 'minions'.'

Jack Bilt straightened like a long, thin pole. He stuck out his neck like a farmyard chicken. 'What would you know about *minions*?' he sneered.

'It's a name for someone's workers,' said Ralph.

Jack gave a slightly startled jump. His left eye twitched. He cocked his head.

'We've done it at school,' Ralph went on. 'Minions are servants. They run around for the boss. A bit like worker ants do for a queen.'

'Ants?' cried Jack, hopping smartly sideways. He got up on his toes and did a little dance, examining the paving stones around his feet.

'The workers are slaves to the queen,' Ralph explained, getting a bit carried away with his favourite subject. He frowned again at Jack. He was getting the oddest feeling that his knowledge of ants was making the builder distinctly uneasy. Jack had a finger hooked under his collar, prising it free of his scrawny neck. Ralph went on, 'Ants are brilliant. Really well organised. Not many people know that ants can carry up to twenty times their own weight—'

'I KNEW,' the builder blasted back. The expulsion of air nearly blew Ralph's hair out. 'And I don't need a cabbage like you to tell me.'

At that moment, the letterbox on Annie's house clattered open. 'Go away, you boys. I know you're out there. I shall call the police. I shall have you all arrested.'

Jack Bilt wheeled round.

'It's all right, Annie. It's only me,' Ralph called. 'There's someone here to look at your house.'

'Oh.' The letterbox fell shut. There was a rattling cascade of locks and chains.

Jack Bilt adjusted his tie and wiped his forehead on the sleeve of his jacket. 'Buzz off,' he hissed from the corner of his mouth.

'I told you, I live here,' Ralph said curtly, stubbing his toe into a drift of leaves. 'I can do what I like.'

Annie Birdlees opened her door.

'Madam!' Jack Bilt leapt forward like a ballet-dancing locust. He plonked his trilby hat on his head and doffed it again, just for Annie's benefit.

'Oh,' said Annie, pulling back, laying one hand across her breast. She looked searchingly at Ralph. He looked helplessly back.

'Delightful house, Mrs—?'

'Birdlees,' Annie said.

'Exquisite,' crooned Jack. 'These Victorian properties. Can't be beaten. Perfect location. Just what I'm after.'

Annie raised a smile, but her mouth was like a meandering stream. 'Erm, have you an appointment, Mr—?'

'Bilt,' said the builder. 'Call me Jack, do.'

'Like the nursery rhyme,' Ralph put in. This was cheeky, he knew, but it was a sort of test. He didn't trust Jack Bilt. He was clearly putting on airs and graces (as his mother might say). If the builder turned and said something obnoxious, maybe Annie would see him for what he really was.

But to Ralph's disappointment, Jack's tone remained as plain as a cream cracker. 'Boys,' he said, with excruciating charm, 'will have their little jokes, won't they, Mrs B?'

Ralph winced. At any moment he expected the builder to lean over the wall, give him ten pence and pat him on the head.

Annie pressed on. 'Did Mr Tattle send you? Only—'

'Tattle?' Jack said. Annie pointed at the sign. 'Ah,' said the builder, 'see what you mean.' He tapped his foot and fed the brim of the trilby quickly through his fingers. 'No. Not sent. On my way to visit my aunt, I was.'

'Oh,' said Annie, quite taken in.

'She's sick. In hospital. Liver. Ghastly business. Skin turning yellow. Fingernails dropping off, one by one.'

'Her fingernails? Oh, how dreadful,' said Annie.

'Could be on her way out,' said Jack.

'The hospital's nowhere near here,' said Ralph.

'I was taking the scenic route,' snapped the builder. He directed his cheesy smile back at Annie. 'Was driving through the Crescent. Saw the sign. Didn't have time to make an appointment. Wondered if I might have a quick peek round?'

'Well...' Annie looked a little uncertain. 'I suppose you could. But if your aunt is poorly and close to passing on, surely you should go to the hospital first?'

'She'll last the weekend,' the builder said, casting a shady glance up the shady Crescent.

Annie thought about it carefully and made up her mind. 'No. I'm sorry. I really think you should come back at a more convenient moment. Please make an appointment with the estate agents. I— oh no...'

As Annie's words tailed off into a mumble, Ralph heard the gentle squeeze of brakes and turned in time to see a cluster of bikes pull up across the road. His body froze.

The Salter gang had arrived in force.

Knocker Makes his Mark

'That's him,' said Kyle to the rest of his 'crew': Jem, Dazza, Callum and Luke.

'Oh,' Annie quivered, looking as if she might be sick in her hands. 'Look out, Mr Bilt. They're pointing at you.'

'Eh?' said Jack.

'This 'iz van!' Luke said, kicking a tyre.

'Bend his aerial,' Dazza whispered.

'Twist his mirror,' Callum said.

Kyle Salter thumped the van hard. 'Oi, this motor's filthy,' he shouted.

'Just like you,' Jem's voice added.

A ripple of laughter bubbled across the road.

Jack Bilt slid his eyes to one side. 'Youths,' he said calmly, reading Annie's fear. 'All this time on their grubby little hands and nothing *constructive* to do with it, have they?'

'They're about to rip your windscreen wipers off,' said Ralph. He was crouching down behind the low privet hedge that shielded his garden from the street.

'You'd better come inside, Mr Bilt,' said Annie.

'Those boys are quite vicious.'

'Delighted,' said Jack, hardly able to believe his luck. 'First, though, better attend to the van.' He looked down at his feet. 'Git up, Knocker.'

Ralph glanced across. He could see the dog now: a white Jack Russell with a light tan face. On its silver studded collar, just under its throat, was some kind of digital bleeper. Jack bent down and fiddled with it a second.

'Mr Bilt,' said Annie, sounding rather anxious, 'you're not going to send that poor thing across to deal with them, are you? They'll squash it. They'll hang it up by its tail.'

'Never underestimate tiny things,' said Jack. Ralph couldn't disagree with that. But a ribby little dog against the entire Salter gang? Kyle would turn it to chunks.

'Oi, look what I've found,' Kyle shouted, flagging a windscreen wiper above his head. He whipped it down on the bonnet of the van. Two wood pigeons fled up Midfield Crescent, clapping their wings as if applauding the shot.

Jack Bilt drew back the cuff of his jacket. On his arm was the strangest-looking gadget that Ralph had ever seen. It had a wrist band, like a watch, but in place of the watch face was some kind of keypad and what appeared to be two diamond-shaped control knobs, flickering red and green beside a silver dial.

'Go,' said Jack. He twisted one diamond. Knocker sped across the road like a furry bullet.

Ralph had never seen a movement like it. There was something very odd about the way the dog ran, something unbalanced. And the noise it made: *knockity, knockity, knockity, knock*.

Dazza was the first to spot the disability. 'What's this?' he howled, doubling up in laughter as Knocker skidded to a kerb-side stop. 'Izzat the best you can *do*? A miniature mutt with a WOODEN LEG?'

Knocker barked and barked. But it didn't seem to Ralph that he was barking at the gang. The dog's nose was almost touching the pavement. A few bright rays of sparkling light seemed to spill from the bleeper on his collar. Then something amazing happened: all the Salter gang started to yelp.

'Ow!' cried Luke. 'Something's bit me foot!'

'What?' said Dazza. Then he was scrabbling off his bike, screaming that he'd had an electric shock. Jemima said her heels were on fire. Callum, on his knees, clutching at his ankle, said the wooden-legged dog must have acid in its spit.

Kyle Salter called them 'ninnies'. He raced towards Knocker with his best boot forward. He was going to have to sort it, as usual, he said. Where dogs and Kyle Salter were concerned, 'sorting' equalled a good hard kicking. Ralph closed his eyes as the bully closed in. Knocker barked once. Kyle swung his foot and…

How he got into the hedge of Number 22, nobody could say. One second he was taking aim on the pavement, about to tuck Knocker into the corner of an imaginary goal, next he was looping back through the air. Double pike with twist. Up. Back. Hedge. Crunch.

'Oh my goodness,' cried Annie, throwing her hands to her face in horror.

'Is it dead?' asked Ralph, opening one eye. To his utter amazement he saw Knocker sitting calmly on the pavement. But where was Kyle?

'W-why did that boy dive into that hedge?' Annie twittered.

'Most odd,' said Jack, lowering the cuff of his jacket again.

'Dive?' said Ralph. 'No one dives into a *hedge*.' But apparently they did. He rubbed his eyes twice to make absolutely sure. Kyle Salter *was* in a hedge – upside down with his head and chest buried and his legs sticking out like a TV aerial. Ralph winced as the members of the Salter gang struggled to drag their leader out. Kyle emerged, looking as if he'd been – well, pulled out of a hedge, backwards. His arms and face were badly scratched. His T-shirt hung in strips from his shoulders. Not surprisingly, he was a little dazed.

'What 'appened?' he groaned. He spat a laurel leaf into the air.

'Dunno,' said Luke.

'It wuz the dog,' said Jem.

'It's a devil dog,' said Callum. 'I'm getting out of it.'

Knocker bared his teeth at the Salter gang and growled. They backed away like puzzled sheep. Devil dog, someone whispered as they left. Knocker reached back and licked his wooden leg.

'Wow...' breathed Ralph.

Jack drew in his lips and gave a 'here boy' whistle. Knocker advanced to the kerb, looked right then left, and knocked sedately back across the road.

'Well,' gasped Annie. She was stunned but uplifted. (Ralph was just stunned.) 'Your little chap certainly showed *them* a thing or two. But whatever happened to his poor back leg?'

Jack wiggled his tie. 'Dreadful business. Industrial

accident. Let's just say the erm...digit is still in the erm...body of the machine.'

'Oh,' squeaked Annie. 'Poor, poor pooch.'

'Done what I can, of course,' Jack said, picking dirt from under his nails. 'Bit of masking tape, elastic and an old broom handle, cut to size. But it's not the same as a good paw, is it? I'd normally reward him with one of his biscuits after a skirmish like that, but I don't always carry them around in the van...'

'Oh, oh,' Annie flapped. 'I think I have a packet of digestives, somewhere.'

'Lovely,' brimmed Jack, gaily rubbing his hands. 'Could manage one myself. While we're looking round the house, perhaps?'

'Oh, err, yes,' said Annie, in a muddled twitter. She looked at Ralph as if to say, 'Is this all right? Am I doing the right thing?' But Ralph was just too shell-shocked to speak. 'I suppose you'd better come in, then, Mr Bilt. I'll put the kettle on. You'd like a cup of tea with your biscuit, I take it?'

'No milk, four sugars, and a dash of brandy.' Jack wiped his feet and swept inside. Knocker barked once and knocked on after him.

Annie, bewildered, blown off course by the rogue gust of wind that was the builder, Bilt, shuffled around and began to close the door. 'Erm, brandy, yes. I think I might have a little left over from Christmas...'

Clunk. The door closed shut.

Ralph swallowed hard.

Jack Bilt had arrived.

A Knock-down Price

'Hedges? Broom handles? Flashing lights? Ralph, you're not making any kind of sense.' Mrs Perfect threw an armful of clothes into the washing machine and set the dial with a determined twist.

Ralph paced the kitchen and tried again. 'But he *did* something, Mum. Mr Bilt, the builder. It was amazing. Kyle Salter ended up in a hedge.'

Mrs Perfect sighed, matching the frequency of the steam cloud issuing from her iron. 'Ralph,' she said impatiently, flapping a shirt across the board, 'throwing people into hedges is neither amazing nor pleasant, even if they are an obnoxious bully.'

'But he didn't, Mum.'

'You just said he did.'

'I know, but…' Oh, it was hopeless, Ralph decided. How could he explain it when it didn't make any sense to him, either? Jack Bilt had been standing a good ten yards away when Kyle had apparently taken off like a rocket and come to earth in a pile of twigs. *Something* must have moved him. Something with incredible strength. But what?

A sudden bang from next door made Ralph lift his head.

'That sounded like Annie's cellar,' said his mum, turning to look at the door to theirs.

The hairs on the back of Ralph's neck began to rise. Jack Bilt in Annie's cellar. Why did Jack, in darkness, make him feel uneasy?

'I expect it's Mr Bilt, having a root around. Checking for damp. That kind of thing.'

Checking, thought Ralph. That's what I should do, check. He cracked his knuckles and headed for the door. 'Going out, Mum.'

'Not far. We'll be eating soon.'

No, not far, Ralph thought. Into next door's garden, that's all.

Annie's back gate was never locked to Ralph. Within seconds he was in her L-shaped garden, creeping past the tubs of flowering shrubs and the hosepipe that never ceased to spit and the bench he had helped to varnish last summer, up past the kitchen to the dining room window that Annie liked to open for a breath of fresh air.

He was in luck. Jack was in the room with his back to the window. Knocker, tongue out and panting, was lying out flat on the blue oval rug in front of the sofa. Annie was pacing back and forth, wringing her gnarled old hands in dismay.

'But I've never had a moment's trouble, Mr Bilt.'

'My sympathies,' said Jack, who sounded more smug than sympathetic to Ralph. 'It's like a sleeping sickness, my dear. Creeps up slowly, then you're engulfed. It wiggles up your brickwork and spreads across your ceilings. Saw a whole ring of these poking out of someone's chimney pot once.' He twiddled a mushroom in his fingers. 'Fungus: starts in the damp, dark places. Cellars. Toilets. Drains. *Shoes.* Spreads like a fog. Checked behind your washing machine lately, have you?'

'Oh,' went Annie, beating her chest. 'This is terrible. Just when I was thinking of selling the house.'

Jack put the mushroom into his pocket. 'Of course, that's not the end of it,' he said, with a grin so oily it could cure a mouse's squeak. He stamped a heel on the polished wooden boards. The thump so startled Ralph that he lost his footing and dislodged a plant pot of fuchsias from a stand. The pot fell with a thud onto softly-turned soil. Another centimetre either way and it would have smashed to pieces on a border-stone.

Knocker was quickly on his feet and growling. Jack

hadn't heard the shuffle outside, but his strange little guard dog had. Letting his twitching nose do the leading, Knocker padded towards the open window. Ralph was about to cut away and run when Jack rasped quietly, 'Git down, Knocker,' and stamped the boards once more. 'Do you hear them?' he asked.

Annie clutched her blouse to her throat in terror.

'Worms,' hissed Jack.

The old dear's eyes almost popped from their sockets.

'Worms that likes to eat wood, my dear.'

'No,' said Annie, cocking her head.

'Takes an experienced ear,' said the builder. He grabbed hold of the rug and whisked it aside. 'If we was to take up a board,' he said, 'the proof would be there in the joists, in the *pudding*.' He pulled a jemmy from inside his jacket. 'Do it for you, but the back's playing up. Old injury, rescuing the dog.' He handed the tool to Annie.

'Oh dear,' she said. 'I couldn't possibly.'

'It's easy,' snapped the builder, eyes shrinking to points. 'Wedge it in a gap and put your weight on it.'

To Ralph's horror, Annie did.

With a snap, and another, a board sprang loose, throwing a rusty brad across the room.

Meanwhile, out of sight of Annie, but not of Ralph, Jack Bilt ordered Knocker into position, then twiddled the strange contraption on his wrist. Ralph saw it clearly: two touches on the red knob, one on the green. Almost immediately, a cloud of fine dust began to pother upwards from the gap in the floor.

'Tut, tut. Worse than I thought,' said Jack. He kicked the board fully out of position and a firework of wood motes shot into the air. 'Look at them go,' he whooped, dancing like a man from the backwoods of America. 'More holes than a Swiss cheese. They're chewing it to bits. They're gobbling it up!'

'Oh, oh, oh,' wailed Annie. 'I've lived here for sixty-seven years. I never knew. Rot and woodworm. Insects and fungi. I can't leave now. Who will give me ninety thousand pounds for this?'

Jack tapped her on the shoulder. 'In stormy times, there's always an umbrella in the rack.' He spat on his palm and held it for her handshake. 'Give you fifty thousand – cash.'

A Strange Discovery

And so the deal was done. Within a fortnight, Annie had packed up and gone and the house next door was no more than a shell, stripped of its furniture (bar an old sofa), awaiting the arrival of the builder, Bilt.

He didn't come immediately. There was a gap of nearly a week, in fact, between Annie's departure and Jack's moving in. And when he did come, the moment was very low key. No removal vans pulling up outside, just the battered white van (still minus one wiper) that Ralph had spotted that first afternoon. Ralph was in the front room, following the afternoon football results, when headlights panned across the TV alcove and there was a slight crunch of wood, as if someone had clipped next door's gatepost with their bumper. He leapt up at once and saw Jack's van pulling onto Annie's drive. Annie's ex-drive. He must get used to that.

'Mum, he's here,' he announced, watching the builder reverse and re-park, this time knocking over a plastic flower urn that Annie had left as a 'housewarming' present. Her good intentions were wasted on Jack, who made no attempt to right it again as he stepped out, slamming his driver's door shut. He flicked a lit cigarette butt onto the lawn, then moved round and opened the van's rear doors, tossing them aside like an old pair of curtains. Ralph felt a growing sense of anxiety as he watched the builder haul out a cardboard box that contained what appeared to be kitchen utensils. A tower of saucepans wobbled and clanked and a lid went crashing towards the ground. A doggy yelp suggested that Knocker had felt the full weight of it.

'Well, what are you waiting for?' said Penny, coming in. She glanced at the envelope balancing on top of the mantelpiece clock. She took it down and handed it to Ralph. 'Go on, and ask him if he'd like a cup of tea.'

Ralph turned the envelope through his hands. Inside it was a 'new home' card, saying: *Welcome to Midfield Crescent from your new neighbours, Ralph and Penny Perfect. If you need anything, please don't hesitate to ask.* Ralph had squirmed when he'd seen the message, and nearly died when he'd been forced to add his signature to that of his mum's. And now, against his better wishes, he had to 'pop round' and pretend to be pleasant – to a man who dropped saucepan lids on his dog and didn't even stop to check if it was hurt.

'Can't *you* do it?' he asked, his toes curling up like

pebbles. 'I don't like him, Mum. He gives me the creeps.'

'Oh, Ralph.' Mrs Perfect glanced through the window as if she might be checking that Jack wasn't listening. The builder was nowhere in sight.

'He does, Mum. He's weird.'

'No, Ralph. He's new. New and different. Why don't you like him?'

Ralph gave an awkward shrug. 'He's got this kind of gadget on his wrist.'

'It's called a watch, Ralph. Lots of people have them.'

'No, Mum. It's special. He does things with it.'

'What kind of things?'

'I'm not sure,' Ralph was forced to admit, fumbling to stay on the left side of logical and the right side of embarrassed. 'I think he controls Knocker with it.'

Mrs Perfect looked at the ceiling. 'Come on,' she sighed, reclaiming the card. 'We'll both go round.'

And half a minute later, there they were.

It hadn't occurred to Ralph that until that moment Jack Bilt had not set eyes on his mother. But he soon became acutely aware of that fact the moment the door to Number 9 swung open. The builder's weedy body gave a surprised start. His mean grey eyes grew big and round. It was a horrible, horrible realisation.

Jack fancied his mother.

That scared Ralph. Big time.

But then, who could blame the builder? For Penelope Jane Perfect was a charming woman. She didn't have the looks of a pop singer or an actress, and she didn't dress in fancy clothes or wear a lot of make-up. A denim jeans and sweater girl, that was what she called herself. A 'girl next door' type, some might say. But her smile was as wide as the ocean was deep, and when it lit up her face, her green eyes sparkled like sunlight dancing on a newly-formed frost. It had melted Jack in a jumping flash.

'Hello, I'm Penelope – Penny – from next door.' She fixed a raft of mousy brown hair into her clip. 'This is Ralph, my son, who I think you've met.'

She tousled Ralph's hair and extended a hand. Jack held it as though it were a piece of lettuce, kissing it with a smoochy smack. 'Enchanted,' he said, leaving a droplet of slobber on her knuckles. 'Mesmerised. Bowled.'

Penny's mouth formed into a rather weak smile. She wiped her hand clean on the waistband of her jeans. 'Thank you,' she said, covering her throat as if she'd spotted a cobra. 'Erm, we just wanted to say hello and give you this.' She elbowed Ralph. He handed out the card.

'Most gracious,' said Jack, pocketing the card without a second glance. His eyes hadn't left Penny's face for an instant.

'Well, we'd better not keep you,' she laughed. 'I'm sure you've got hundreds of things to be doing.' She backed away, miming juggling movements. 'If there's anything you need, don't hesitate to ask. Come along, Ralph.'

'Hundreds,' Jack said, when they were halfway down the path.

Ralph bumped to a halt at his mother's back.

'Pardon?' she said.

'And thousands,' Jack added. 'Need some of those.'

'Hundreds and thousands?' Penny repeated.

Jack licked his lips with a paper-thin tongue. 'Sugary beads. All the colours of the rainbow. Very tasty. Very sustaining.'

Penny looked at him oddly. 'Are you making a trifle?'

Jack's eyes dipped. 'Find them a valuable food source,' he said, in a whisper so sinister that Ralph shuddered hard and almost lost his balance. Knocker, sitting just behind Jack, growled. 'Like a spoonful or two in my tea.'

A sprig of hair worked loose over Penny's brow. She blew it, half-heartedly, making it dance. 'Well, yes, I think I have a tub in the pantry.'

'And scrubbers,' said Jack, making scrubbing movements.

Penny thought for a moment. 'You mean scouring pads?'

'I do,' said Jack. 'Soft on the one side, wiry on the other.'

Penny smiled a little uncomfortably. 'Yes, I've got a new pack under the sink. I'll send Ralph round with them in a few minutes.'

Minutes, thought Ralph and glanced at Jack's wrist. The device was covered by the builder's sleeve. This was his chance. While Mum could see. 'What time is it?' he asked.

'Uh?' Jack grunted.

'Have you got the time, please?' Ralph repeated.

There was a pause, then his mother guessed what he was up to. 'Oh, pay no attention to Ralph, Mr Bilt. He knows the time; he just wants a closer look at your watch. He thinks it's some strange science-fiction device that allows you to remotely control your dog!'

'How comical,' said Jack, smiling limply. And yet his hand spread guardedly over his wrist.

'Books,' said Penny. 'That's his trouble. Reads too many books.'

'Why does it blink so much?' asked Ralph, who felt

there was no harm in reading lots of books. It made you inquisitive. It helped you learn. It made you want to challenge a dubious character like Mr Jack Bilt of Midfield Crescent.

Jack lifted his sleeve. Ralph locked his gaze firmly on the device. Not diamonds. Pyramids. He'd misread the shape of the flashing 'jewels'. But not the colour. One green one (lit). One red one (not). And round the side of the casing a few buttons and keys. What did they do, though? What did they do?

'It's a particle displacement device,' said Jack.

Penny Perfect spluttered with laughter. Knocker whimpered and tapped his stick. Ralph moved back half a pace.

Jack crept forward like a creature of the dark. 'If I so desired,' he said, 'I could wobble his molecules and shrink him to the size of half my thumb. Would he be more use to you like that, my dear?'

He turned the device in Ralph's direction. An aerial slid from the side of the casing. The red pyramid lit. The green one flickered. Figures flashed across the silver dial. A surge of fear made Ralph cry, 'No!'

'Oh, Ralph,' laughed Penny. 'He's teasing you.'

Jack tapped a button.

Ralph covered his face.

There was a beep – and Jack said: 'At the third stroke, it will be ten past six.' He pointed to the dial. Floating at its centre were the numerals 18:10. Ten past six. The right time, more or less.

Penny Perfect hooted with laughter.

Ralph crossed his arms and felt completely humiliated. So, Jack Bilt had a black sense of humour. Ralph hated him all the more for that.

'We really must go,' said Penny, 'just in case you're telling the truth, Mr Bilt!'

'Jack,' he said, with piano keys for teeth.

Penny crouched down and coochied Knocker. 'Is that how you got so little, eh? Did your molecules get a bit wobbled?' The little Jack Russell jerked in surprise. *Not used to kindness*, thought Ralph. But the dog was responding to his mother's touch, nuzzling her palm, seeking the affection.

'Such a shame about his leg,' she said.

'He gets by,' said Jack, without a shred of compassion.

Ralph glanced at the missing 'digit' and his heart took its biggest, most fearful leap yet. For what he'd assumed to be a chewed-off stump, a piece of doggy gristle left hanging in place by the jaws of a machine, was nothing of the kind. It was…

He was leaning in for a closer look when Jack slapped

a hand to his chest and said, 'Knocker wants feeding. Time you was off.'

Ralph stared into the builder's needle-quick eyes. Too late, you know I've seen it, he thought.

There *was* a leg on Knocker.

There was.

It was shrivelled to the size of half a thumb.

A Plumber Calls

The next morning began with an argument.

'Well, I don't know which is worse,' said Penny, spreading marmalade around with such slap and such dash that Ralph had to lean back on his stool to avoid being splattered with slapdashed spots. 'It's either disabled or a mutant. Which would you prefer?'

Disabled or a mutant? The thought was enough to make Ralph shrivel. 'You don't understand, Mum. Jack said Knocker's leg had been chopped by a machine. But it hasn't. It's there. It's just withered up. That means he was lying.'

Mrs Perfect gave a maternal sigh. 'Ralph, it really doesn't matter *how* the poor animal came to be in that state, it just is. What it needs is love and affection, like any living creature. The fact that Mr Bilt bothers to keep it at all is a sign that he's got a caring heart.'

Poink. A plate of toast arrived on the table with all the heat of a spacecraft re-entering the thin kitchen atmosphere.

Ralph felt it was time to make his point. He had his *Star Trek* pants on; he went for it, boldly: 'Unless he miniaturised it with his special watch and he's got to keep Knocker so that no one will discover his wicked secret!'

Penny Perfect placed a hand to her forehead. There was marmalade on her fingers and now in her hair. (Ralph didn't have the heart to tell her.) 'Oh yes, silly me. How could I have missed the obvious option? Mr Bilt is really an evil scientist, so dastardly that he's prepared to carry out hideous experiments on his dog!'

'Yes!' cried Ralph, pleased they were getting somewhere at last.

Prok. A mug of tea followed the toast to its landing site. 'I was joking,' his mother said darkly.

'But—' Ralph started, when the doorbell rang. He reluctantly decided to save his jaw for the other important purpose of the morning: breakfast.

Mrs Perfect headed for the door.

'Sorry to disturb you,' came a breezy male voice. 'I'm after your neighbour. Would you know if he's about?'

Ralph was off the blocks quicker than an Olympic sprinter.

'You mean Mr Bilt?' asked Penny, anticipating Ralph's arrival with a well-timed, well-placed palm to his forehead, buffering him like a troublesome toddler.

'That's it,' said the man, smiling at Penny's handling

of Ralph. 'Dangerous is he, if he gets out?'

Embarrassed, Ralph glared at the man. He was tall and handsome and probably quite muscular, though it was difficult to tell through his dark-blue boiler suit. He had his hands in his pockets and a tabloid newspaper under one arm. By his feet was a metal toolbox. He was a workman of some kind. In the building trade, perhaps? That set Ralph's nerves tick-ticking again. Was the visitor a mate of Jack's? Another member of the evil gang?

The caller explained his business. 'Tom Jenks. Plumber. Mr Bilt needs one urgently, apparently. I'm due to see him at ten, but I'm a little early. Wondered if he might be with you, that's all. Obviously not. No worries. I'll sit outside in the van and wait.' He turned away.

Penny Perfect let out a hesitant, 'Oh.'

Tom Jenks stopped and looked back at her for a moment.

'You're welcome to come in and have a cup of tea, if you like?' The hinges creaked as she changed the angle of the door to 'friendly'.

Tom Jenks billowed the pockets of his suit.

And just for a second, a millisecond perhaps, Ralph noticed that his mother's eyes widened a little. She stroked her neck as Tom said, 'Love to', then pampered her hair and seemed terribly flustered to find a sticky patch of marmalade gelling up her fringe.

Flustered and red. Unmistakable signs. His mother liked Tom Jenks.

Fair enough, thought Ralph. He'd rather have the plumber's happy blue eyes instead of the ominous chips of flint that were such a feature of their next-door neighbour. He shut the door and hurried to the kitchen.

His mother was already in kettle mode, tea bags and mugs appearing like magic. She was going for the biscuits, the *chocolate* ones, no less, when her industry abruptly stopped short. Falling back against the sink, with her fingers steepled to her mouth she said, 'Actually, could I be extraordinarily cheeky and ask you a favour?'

Ralph studied Tom Jenks and could tell by the growing admiration in his eyes that he'd probably do anything for Penny just then.

'The tap drips,' he said, short-circuiting his mother's request.

'Ralph!' she snapped, crossing her arms in a protective fashion (as if *that* would stop her face glowing red). 'That might not have been what I was going to ask.'

Well, it's a bit too soon for a date, Ralph thought,

though saying that would have seen him grounded for a year. He shrugged and looked at the grinning Tom Jenks.

With surprising confidence, Tom bracketed his hands around Penny's arms and gently moved her away from the sink. 'Mmm, that's going to cost you,' he murmured.

'Oh dear,' she sighed, 'how much exactly?'

'Cup of tea *and* a biscuit, I reckon.'

Penny blushed triumphantly and emptied half a pack of bourbons onto a plate.

Mr Jenks opened the under-sink cupboard and knelt down to turn off the cold water stopcock. 'Hello, you've got an ant in here.' He surfaced with it, dancing on his hand.

'Don't squash it,' said Ralph.

'Wouldn't dream of it,' said Tom. He opened the back door and put the creature out.

Ralph smiled at his mum, who lifted an eyebrow. Now that made two of them who liked Tom Jenks.

'So,' the plumber stated boldly, somehow managing to whistle and talk and eye up Penny's figure (and plumb) all at once, 'what's your theory on this house that's gone missing?'

'House?' said Penny, arranging the bourbons in an artistic fan.

'Front-page news,' said Tom. He nodded at the paper as he clamped the cold tap and wrenched it loose. 'Whole thing disappeared over the weekend, somewhere up in a remote part of Yorkshire. Uninhabited, derelict place. Not a brick left. Paper reckons it was abducted by aliens.'

'A house?' repeated Penny.

'Aliens?' echoed Ralph. 'Why would aliens steal a house?'

'Seen the price of property on Mars?' Tom quipped.

Ralph scowled at the joke and looked at his mum. Together, they turned the paper around. On the front was a picture of a muddy field. A bemused policeman was standing in a puddle on the spot where the house had allegedly been. In the background, two sheep were looking on dumbly. The headline simply read: SPIRITED AWAY.

'But that's ridiculous,' said Penny, shaking her head. 'A house can't just disappear like that.'

'Could if there's a gang on the job,' said Tom.

Ralph shuffled his chair. The word 'gang' made him think of Kyle Salter. What had happened to Kyle, he wondered? Like the mysterious missing house, the bully hadn't been seen for some time.

'Twenty or thirty able blokes could take it down in no

time, I reckon. Stack it up on lorries, brick by brick, then drive it away under cover of darkness. It'll turn up as Lego in an aircraft hangar or a hay barn, you'll see.'

'But why?' asked Penny. 'What's the point?'

Tom shrugged his broad blue shoulders. 'Prank, I expect. Someone, somewhere, must be having a good giggle.' He clanked the tap and a fountain of water bubbled out of the joint. 'Aha, there's your culprit.' He dug out a washer with a screwdriver blade, then rattled around in his box for a new one. Within seconds it was fitted and the leak was fixed.

'Thank you,' said Penny. 'You're very kind.'

'No problem,' said Tom. He sat down and took a bourbon.

Ralph drummed his fingers on the table top. 'Do you believe in aliens?' he asked.

'Oh, Ralph,' said his mum.

'Not really,' laughed Tom. 'I do believe in ghosts, though. I saw one once, in my grandma's kitchen, washing socks on an old scrubbing board. Whoever stole that house could be in for a shock. According to the paper, it was haunted.'

'Oh,' went Penny, touching her heart.

She jumped as a door banged shut somewhere.

'That sounds like Mr Bilt returning,' said Tom.

'Unless you're hiding a ghost as well?'

Penny forced her lips into a wobbly smile, making Ralph wonder what had troubled her the most: the idea of a wailing ghost or the disappointment that Tom would soon be on his way.

The plumber stood up. He popped two biscuits into his pocket and drank his tea like a man with a dragon's furnace for a throat. 'Mr Bilt says there's quite a bit of work to be done, so I expect we'll see each other again.'

'Oh, yes, I expect we will,' said Penny, diverting her eyes from his face to the floor. She gave her hands work to do, tidying the table. 'We'll look forward to that, won't we, Ralph?'

'Yes,' said Ralph, who felt sure that in Tom Jenks he'd have a strong ally in his quest to investigate Mr Jack Bilt.

But as the plumber clanked his tools down the hall once more, neither Ralph nor his mother could possibly have guessed at the strangeness to come. When Tom Jenks waved his fond goodbye, little did they know it was the last they would see of him for quite some time.

Like Kyle Salter and the house in Yorkshire, the plumber was about to completely disappear.

Here Comes Old Nick

Stop.

Let's take a moment here to step inside the mind of young Ralph Perfect. What must be going through his busy brain now? A brain enlivened by the world of books ever since it discovered that wonderful ability to turn words into magical moving pictures. What must such a boy, his imagination stirred by all that he has seen, be making of his slightly sinister neighbour?

First, there is still no explanation for the spring-heeled dive of the odious Kyle Salter. How *did* that bully get into that hedge? Did Jack release some strange kind of force field? Some hidden energy? Some untapped power as yet undescribed by the laws of physics? Or is his strange dog, Knocker, truly an agent of the devil, Beelzebub? Did it bark and cast a transforming spell that heaved the bully high into the air? Or was it merely that Kyle was scared out of his pants and leapt a little further from trouble than expected?

The mind boggles. Particularly Ralph's.

And what of the woodworm devouring Annie's joists? Since witnessing that peculiar phenomenon, Ralph, inquisitive soul that he is, has surfed the outer limits of the internet for answers. He has looked up every genus of wood-boring beetle that munched its way through the Ark (two by two), but nowhere has he read that these creatures could carve up a sturdy beam of wood with the force of a dozen high-powered drills, making clouds and clouds of motes in the process. Somehow, Annie had been tricked. Tricked into believing her house was falling down. Tricked into giving up her home too cheaply. So if nothing else, Jack Bilt is a fraud and a thief.

And Knocker. What about that leg of his? So perfectly formed and yet so tiny. This irregular canine anomaly has been rapping Ralph's forehead from the inside out. Ralph is fully aware, of course, that certain human people have suffered disabilities similar to this. He once saw a man in the local shopping centre with a normal body but arms the size of a newborn baby. His mother had explained explicitly to him that this was the wretched side-effect of a drug treatment now no longer in use. Consider, then, the whirrings and stirrings in the darkest corners of Ralph's imagination when he sees that stunted leg on Knocker. Has the dog been forced to take a drug? Has his mother, Penny, stumbled on the truth in naming Jack as some evil kind of scientist? A demented doctor? A modern Viktor Frankenstein? A madman who lives on hundreds and thousands?

What on earth is going on in the house next door?

Why, for instance, is it so, so quiet? Since the day Ralph popped round with a small pack of scouring pads (and promptly had the door closed hard in his face), hardly a squeak has been heard from next door. No sounds of unpacking. No TV. No music. Had it not been for the toilet, flushing, Ralph might have been forgiven for thinking Jack was dead.

And spying from the garden was impossible now. For there were blue sheets hanging in the large bay windows. No curtains. No lace. Just ugly, plastic sheets that in all probability had 'keep-out' watermarked on their surface. Whatever was going on within those walls, Jack Bilt had no intention of the world outside knowing anything about it.

But Ralph had seen things. Lots of things. Bell jars. Yes, there were definitely bell jars. The glasses of science. The vessels of chemistry. Ralph had seen Jack carrying them in. Usually at night, when Midfield Crescent was cloaked in mist and owls were hooting and mice were scurrying and bats were occasionally seen flitting through the lamplight. Without binoculars or a suitable pirate eyeglass, it had been impossible to see inside the jars. But with a mind like Ralph's, who needed binoculars? There were specimens in the jars, he was sure of it. Experimental samples. Foul tests. Strangely-contorted unfamiliar creatures floating in soupy straw-coloured fluids that would sting your eyes when the lids were removed. All hidden in the cellar, tucked under the house. Deep in the darkness where the mushrooms grow.

Specimens.

Tests.

Jars.

And a fish tank. A fish tank, yes. Jack had dragged it from the back of his van one night and immediately thrown a blanket across it. He had staggered down the path with the tank in his arms, stumbling over the bags of sweating rubbish that were stacking up outside Annie's once-loved door, cursing poor Knocker for getting under his feet.

A fish tank. Covered up and carted inside. Fish? Why? Jack doesn't seem the type to be keeping guppies.

And now comes the biggest mystery of all: what has happened to the plumber, Tom Jenks? A fortnight has passed since the tap was fixed and the bourbons were slipped into the pocket of his boiler suit, and not a clank of his tools has been heard in the Crescent. All the grand and merry expectations that Ralph and his mother had constructed for the plumber have dripped like the tap and slowly run dry. Excuses have been found, illnesses suggested. But now, disappointment is all that fills their hearts.

Until this morning, when another new face appears in the Crescent. A thick-necked, small feather duster of a man. Suited but dishevelled. Loafers on his feet. Wispy grey hair and a peppery moustache. A man you might say at first glance was an oaf, an idiot escaped from the village up the road. But looks can be deceptive; this man is not an oaf. He has eyes like a hawk. They are used to solving mysteries.

He also has a name. And a most impressive title.

Detective Inspector Nicholas Bone.

Known to his comrades in the force as 'Old Nick'.

When the doorbell spilt its note up the stairs, Ralph was on his bed with his head wrapped up in the world of Jack. Something else had occurred to him: he hadn't seen the builder build a single thing. No hammers hammering, no saws buzzing, no concrete mixers churning slop. Not even a trademark radio blaring. The blackbirds in the garden had been more industrious. Spiders had webbed. Snails had shelled. Ants had built colonies deep underground. But Jack had not lifted so much as a plumb bob. Was it, then, a cover? Did he call himself a builder to avoid attention? How far would an evil scientist go?

'Ralph, can you come downstairs a moment?' His mother's voice dragged him to the front door.

The visitor wiggled his moustache at the boy.

'This is Inspector Bone,' said Penny. 'He's a policeman, Ralph. He wants to ask some questions about Mr Jenks. Do you remember Mr Jenks? Tom, the plumber?'

'Yes,' said Ralph. Of course he remembered. Why was his mother looking so pale?

'Do you want to come in?' she said.

'No, thank you,' DI Bone replied in a voice as thick as tomato purée. His accent lay somewhere to the south and west. Somerset, maybe. The Mendip Hills. He stepped backwards and looked at the house next door. 'It's this chap, Bilt, I've really come to talk to. Can't seem to raise him. Wondered if he might be with you, that's all?'

Ralph saw his mother gulp. Wasn't this what Tom had said the day he'd arrived? 'No,' she said, her voice cracking with undisguised worry. 'Is Tom all right? He came here to do some work two weeks ago.'

Bone studied the upstairs windows of the house, a cupped hand blotting the sun from his eyes. 'Yes, I know. It was written in his diary. The first of three calls he was due to make that day.'

Due to make? Penny scrunched her top into her trembling fist.

'The day he disappeared,' the policeman added, just as the door to Jack's house burst open.

'Ah,' said Bone, nipping smartly round the party wall to face the builder. 'Mr Bilt? Been knocking your door for several minutes. Thought for a moment you were trying to avoid me.'

'Ablutions,' said Jack. 'Even Her Majesty has a small throne.' He slanted his dark eyes sideways at Ralph.

'Quite,' said Bone and flashed a police identity card. He then asked Jack if he'd seen a Thomas Peter Jenks in these parts? He showed a picture of the plumber. A family picture: Tom cuddling a child, a dog at their feet. This turned Ralph's stomach and made his mother gulp. They'd seen it on the telly, this kind of thing.

'Ah,' Jack said, with a grisly sneer. He dragged a broken-toothed comb through his lanky hair. 'I do remember him. Course I do. Quoted me a price for some boiler work. Sky high, it was. Astrobloomin'nomical. Didn't take him on. Didn't like him much. Made jokes about the dog. Very unpleasant.'

No, thought Ralph. That didn't sound right. The Tom he'd met wouldn't hurt an ant. He'd have pitied Knocker.

DI Bone smiled tight-lipped at the terrier. 'Mind if I take a look inside?'

Yes! Ralph cracked his knuckles in triumph. Now the evil would surely be uncovered. His mother tutted and nudged him hard, Tone it down, will you? But Ralph could see in her soft, green eyes that she was secretly wanting this too.

But if Ralph was expecting the wily builder to make a sudden run for it up the Crescent, he was about to be sorely disappointed. Jack, instead, did a very odd thing. Raising his arms until his undersized jacket lifted out like a pair of wings, he said, 'You can frisk me if you like.'

Hrow, went Knocker, as if posing the question none of the humans dared to ask: why? Why would Jack invite a copper to check his pockets?

Double bluff, thought Ralph. He blurted out: 'Do it.'

'Ralph?!' His mother took the opposite view.

So did Old Nick. 'I don't think that will be necessary,' he said.

Jack shrugged and seemed a little disappointed. With a sweep of his hand he invited Bone in.

Five minutes later, the policeman came out.

Ralph was in the street, pretending to be sweeping up fallen leaves. He heard Bone say, 'Thank you. I shouldn't think we'll need to bother you again.' And down the path he came, flapping his tie like the tail of a kipper. 'Bye, son,' he said, as he got into his car.

'What did you find?' Ralph gibbered. He was staggered to see the detective leaving without Jack Bilt cuffed firmly to his arm.

'An old sofa, a week's worth of washing-up, an aquarium, some pot plants, a cuddly toy. Why?'

Ralph wasn't sure. He blabbed something out. 'Tom said there'd be a lot of work next door.'

The detective nodded. 'Looks like your neighbour's going to gut the place and sell it on at a handsome profit. Unless he turns it into a house of mirrors. The house that Jack Bilt. There's one for you.'

'But where's Tom?' Ralph bleated.

Bone slammed his door shut. His electric window glided down. 'That, I don't know. But I'm working on it. Sometimes people just take off, son, for reasons only they can answer.'

Up went the window again.

But you can't just leave, thought Ralph. Jack's evil. Didn't you see his vile experiments? Or ask about his watch? Or check Knocker's leg? You're a detective. You can't trust a man who sugars his tea with hundreds and thousands. Didn't you at least go into the cellar?

The car roared into the distance.

Right, that does it, Ralph thought. He turned and glared at the blue plastic sheets. Now there was only one thing for it. He was going to have to get inside and snoop around himself.

Breaking In

It came to him in a flash, the way to break in. Doors and windows were difficult and criminal. What he had to do was think like a small thing: like an ant. Ants were no respecters of boundaries. Where there was a crack, they made for it. Where there was a weakness, they dug and dug until a passage opened up.

Cracks.

Boundaries.

Think like an ant.

Flash. Ralph knew the perfect place.

The cellar. He was going to make a hole in the cellar wall.

His mother had once told him that the walls of these houses were 'paper thin'. She meant there was only one course of brickwork separating their house from that next door. And Ralph knew for a fact that at the far end of the cellar, in the large, airy space that ran under the lounge, the wall was not just paper thin, but crumbling. Put a finger in the mortar between the rows of bricks and you could scrape out damp sand as easily as you pleased. Scrape away enough and a brick would come loose. Remove enough bricks and you had a hole. Make a hole and you had a passage. Crawl through the passage and you had the answers.

It was as easy as that.

As easy as waiting for Jack to go out…then complaining that you couldn't find your roller blades anywhere.

'I can't find my roller blades, anywhere, Mum!'

'They're in the cellar,' she said, 'with all your other junk. If you took the trouble to clear it like I've asked, then—'

She never finished the sentence. Ralph was already down the steps and shouting, 'OK, OK, don't go on. I'll *do* it.'

It was really no trouble at all.

He flicked on the light: a single bulb on a dodgy-looking wire that smelt of years of toasted dust. It was creepy in here, in the belly of the house. Dampness clung like a fine moist film and your nostrils soon became hopelessly clogged with the cloying scent of paint-brush cleaner and the sweat from a pair of faded wellies. Mum used to tell him when he was little that his gran would come here to feed biscuits to the dragon, because if you didn't the house would not be warmed. The 'dragon' Ralph discovered at the age of nine, was an old gas meter and the 'biscuits', coins. Although the meter had been long since disconnected, something called a shilling still sat on top of it, just to keep the fire of the dragon burning. There was no dragon present at the moment, just a niggling breeze from the bare space surrounding the conduit of a gas main, stabbing Ralph's neck like a vampire's bite.

He found his roller blades right away. What was clutter to mums was organised chaos to boys like him. He plucked them off the rusting, oil-filled radiator that Mum had refused to send to the tip in case of 'unexpected dragon emergencies' and hid them inside the battered, leather case, which had not seen daylight for the past three years and was now a hidey hole for woodlice and mould. This was a ploy to keep him here longer, just in case Mum popped her head into the cellar.

For several minutes he did tidy up, not with any thoughts of making it easier to locate anything, but just to carve a path between the mops, brooms, wine-making equipment, buckets, tools, paint cans and paste board, an old hamster cage, the leather football he'd never inflated (and the pump he should have inflated it with), endless pieces of skirting board, the bathroom mirror he'd cracked with a toffee hammer and his mum wouldn't throw out for fear of bad luck. He parted it all like Moses at the Red Sea, until the far wall, Jack's wall, was cleared of everything but cobwebs and whitewash.

Ralph prodded a likely-looking brick. It moved – only a fly's wing, granted, but the avalanche of sand it produced was spectacular. He found a small chisel from the toolbox on the shelf and quietly began to scrape.

The first brick came out like a baby's tooth, bringing a spike of cold air with it. Ralph sucked the chill deep down into his lungs. It wriggled and turned inside his air sacs, forcing a dry cough out of his throat. It felt like a warning not to continue, as if some mummy was walled up here and its burial place was cursed with a death cloud. Ralph covered his mouth and shone a torch through the hole. Something glinted. Glass, perhaps? Through a gap this small it was impossible to see. He switched off the torch and struck the next brick.

His intention was to take out twenty. That was what he thought his body would require: a gap four across and five layers down, a hole that wouldn't take long to rebuild. But after twelve or so bricks he stopped and jumped back when two fell out of their own accord and a row of stone blocks just above his head made a frightening, grinding noise. If the house collapsed, he was going to be in trouble (and horribly squashed). So he stacked the last bricks on the pile beside the meter and played the torch into the hole again.

Surprisingly, the light did not travel far, but struck what appeared to be a large, vertical cardboard box (he reached through and tapped it lightly), which was propped at an angle against Jack's wall. It was blocking out the major part of the hole, which meant he could squeeze through under cover.

Cool.

But squeezing was easier imagined than done. Head and shoulders went through well enough, but teetering on his tummy with his feet off the ground and nothing to grab onto on the other side was a bad fall waiting to happen...

Crunch.

He landed on the cold, damp floor next door, rolled and banged his head on the cardboard thing (it was surprisingly firm). His hair and sweater were now full of 'gubbins' (as his mother would say). An explanation would have to be invented, but he'd think about that once his foray was done. Right now, he needed to see Jack's cellar.

With fear springing shoots in every pore of his body, he peered into the deepest depths of the crypt. It was surprisingly empty. Frighteningly empty. Frustratingly empty. No vats. No cages. No phials of frothing liquid. No chains. No skeletons. No scientific *instruments*. Nothing. Just a strong smell of damp and a pair of wooden shelves.

Sturdy white shelves – with jars on them.

Tall bell jars. A little run of them reflected the torch beam back. The beam flickered. Went out. Ralph panicked and struck the torch against his thigh. It flickered again, not unlike his nerves. Stupid batteries. He must work fast.

He hurried to the jars, raising the light to a large one on the end. There was a miniature oak tree inside it, standing up on its tangled roots. Ralph frowned in thought. He had seen small trees several times before when he'd mooched around garden centres with his mum. Bonsai, they were called. Japanese people liked to grow them. But this tree didn't really look like one of those. It wasn't in a tray of soil for a start. Its leaves and acorns were withered and dropping, and there was a tiny, grey object among its branches. Ralph trained the light harder. Ugh! It was a squirrel.

He tried the next jar along. There was an old, red telephone kiosk in it.

In the jar next to that was a double-decker bus.

Something seriously weird was going on here.

He dipped to the shelf below. Here was something he hadn't seen Jack unloading: sweet jars, four of them, hidden in the shadows. He checked the first. It appeared to be filled with fluff. Fluff? Why would Jack keep a jar of *fluff*?

In the next was some vaguely orange-coloured goo that made huge smears up the sides of the glass.

In the next were thousands of toenail clippings. Probably some from fingers, too.

With a squeak of disgust, Ralph turned and walked towards the hole in the wall. That was it. He was going home. What kind of freak kept nails in a jar? And…oh! His hand shot up to his mouth as it occurred to him now what the fluff could be: tummy fluff, dug from Jack Bilt's *button*, and the orange stuff was probably ear wax. And the fourth jar? No. He didn't want to know.

But now came a find even more disturbing: the truth about the cardboard box. As he stumbled against it he saw the shape properly.

It was a coffin, propped up against the wall.

There was a lidless coffin in Jack Bilt's cellar.

In the House

At this moment, Ralph had choices. First there was the very sensible choice, which was to scrabble back through the hole he'd made, rebuild the wall (no matter how loosely), retrieve his roller blades from the old suitcase, turn off his torch, dust himself down, hurry upstairs to his loving mum, shut the cellar door and *never* think of Jack Bilt *ever* again. *Ever.*

And then there was the not-so-sensible choice.

This one is not so easy to describe, for it draws upon that twitching inquisitiveness that seems to be at the root of every young person's mind. That ticklish seed of deep curiosity which makes a boy determined to plant his feet, grit his teeth and say to himself, 'No. I will be brave. I have come this far, I will not be defeated. I will go on and discover the truth. Hurrah.'

(Comes of reading too many adventure stories, perhaps?)

Whatever the reason, the not-so-sensible choice is the one Ralph took. He gritted his feet and planted his teeth (or something like that) and shone his torch right over that coffin. Was it possible? Was it really possible that Jack was a vampire who slept in the cellar – at an upright angle? Ralph tutted and shook his head. Of course not. Now he was just being stupid. Vampires only came out at night, and he'd seen Jack walking in blazing sunlight. Any blood-sucking creature of darkness would have gone up in smoke at the first bright ray. Unless Jack was a new breed of vampire? What if he'd developed a special type of sun block, made from the ear wax he kept in that jar? Ugh. It didn't bear thinking about, rubbing *ear wax* into your skin. That was too gross, even for a vamp. He trained his light on the coffin again. Was it possible to tell if a coffin, like a bed, had been recently slept in? He put his hand inside it and touched the base. Something immediately scuttled through his fingers. With a yelp he pulled away.

A woodlouse tumbled onto the floor.

Perfect, steel yourself, he thought. Be a boy of iron. Take three deep breaths then sneak through the door at the top of the cellar steps – and snoop.

He took six deep breaths. It made him dizzy, but in a few woozy strides he was at the cellar door. The handle was loose and rattled as he turned it. If Jack or Knocker was on the other side… Dry-mouthed, he pressed his ear to the panels. Nothing. You could have heard a ghost sleepwalking out there. He opened the door and stepped into the hall.

It was cold and dead. Dead in the sense of dark and unwelcoming. Even Annie's taste in floral wallpapers could do nothing to improve the gloom. He tiptoed to the front room and switched on the light.

The place was a tip, far worse than Inspector Bone had described it. There were unwashed cups on every surface (some growing layers of green mould and fungus), socks and pants and other bits of clothing sitting in a heap beside the fire, a bowl of cold porridge on the arm of the sofa and piles of old newspapers strewn across the floor. The loose board Annie had crowbarred out still lay, bottom up, on top of its neighbour. Cold air was blowing through the open gap. It was creepy, bizarre. How could anyone, even Jack, survive in such a dump? The only shred of comfort was the two-cushion sofa. But even that was covered with dog hairs and tobacco and powdered with splashes of cigarette ash. On the floor beside the hearth sat Knocker's dog bowl, also unwashed and visited by flies. Next to it, a dented watering can. Ralph couldn't see the point of that. The only plants in the room were a bunch of ferns in a large ceramic pot and they were turning brown with dehydration. Looking round, there were only three things of serious interest: a cluster of shopping bags huddled in the bay; a single wardrobe minus its door; and just beneath the window from where he'd done his spying, a flimsy trestle table, bowed at its centre, supporting an object that was covered by the same blue plastic sheeting shutting out the light from both main windows.

Eeny, meeny, miny, mo: he went to the bags.

To his disappointment, they were filled with tools. Trowels, chisels, clamps, hammers, an electric drill, a spirit level. Ralph clicked his teeth and stood away. Tools were the trademark of a proper builder. And all of these items bore the scratches and batterings of extended use. So Jack wasn't lying about his profession? But why carry his kit in plastic bags? Why not a toolbox?

Another mystery.

He turned to the wardrobe that wasn't. There were no shelves and no hanging rail as well as no door. But up the inside walls were two tall columns of coloured light bulbs, which made it look like a cheap magician's cabinet. Ralph thought about stepping inside it. But he knew about children who stepped into wardrobes: they met lions and witches on the other side. So he circled it warily, knocking the wood. As far as he could tell, it had no mirrors, levers or hidden panels, but on the floor of the cabinet he did find something.

A tiny white van.

It was lying on its side when Ralph picked it up, as though cast away by a spoilt child. There was a bright blue logo across the back doors, but the words had blurred into the sweep of the design, making it impossible to read a name. The same was true of the number plates. Elsewhere, however, the detail was stunning. Especially underneath, where it was possible to trace the silver exhaust pipe all the way up into the engine manifold. You could even see rust on the big box silencer. And when Ralph opened the driver's door (by actually turning a handle down), he was amazed to see a minute orange lunchbox tumble off the passenger seat, into the foot well of the cab. A pair of microscopic furry dice were dangling from the rear view mirror. A map book was wedged into a pocket of the door. Ralph had kept many toy cars in his time, but never one quite as lifelike as this. To his shame, he was tempted to steal it. But the urge soon passed and all he did was set the van down on its impressively realistic tyres and move across to the trestle table. Gingerly, he lifted one corner of the sheet.

The side of a fish tank came into view.

Inside the tank was a very small house.

Ralph thought, at first, he was peeping at a dolls'

house. But it wasn't made of plywood, and it wasn't a toy. It had brick walls blackened by chimney smoke, battlements, gargoyles, a weed-ridden flight of concrete steps with lion statues at either side, and a turret with a pointed top. Ivy was creeping round broken, shuttered windows. Water was dripping from a leaking gutter. Slates were missing from the bowing roof. There was even a small horse chestnut tree growing out of the narrow strip of earth which surrounded the house like a filled-in moat. It was just as if Jack had uprooted the place from a model village and planted it here.

But why put a house inside a fish tank?

Without any water?

Without any fish?

When it didn't even look like a sunken castle?

At the side of the tank lay a magnifying glass. Ralph stared at it blankly. It never occurred to him to pick it up and look at the house more closely. Instead, his gaze drifted to the corner of the table, where the tub of hundreds and thousands was sitting, kept like fish flakes by the aquarium.

He didn't have time to ask himself why. At that moment, he heard a sound that set his vertebrae rattling like a row of falling dominoes. A clicking, twisty, metallic sort of snap. The snap a key makes when it half-turns in a lock.

Jack.

Jack was home.

JACK!

Ralph dropped the plastic sheet and ran: out of the front room, straight into the kitchen. One supposes that it must have been the terror that addled him, but yes, he missed the cellar door completely. By the time this error had registered in his brain, it was far too late to double back. Knocker's leg was tapping out its rhythm in the hall. Jack's hacking cough was only just behind.

He dived for the door to the garden. The glass panes shuddered as he worked the handle. A chip of dried putty hit the floor. A shocked sparrow fluttered from its water bath outside. But that kitchen door simply would not budge.

In the hall, Knocker stopped knocking. Ralph heard a growl building in the dog's throat. The terrier had heard him or smelt his fear. Knocker knew that mischief was afoot.

'Git out the way,' Jack said, coughing.

Knocker yapped.

Ralph's temples pulsed.

Closer, closer the knocking came. The three-legged doggy was heading for the kitchen.

Now there was only one way out.

At the rear of the kitchen was a downstairs toilet. Annie, dear Annie, had used it all the time, rather than climb the stairs to the modern one. A couple of years ago, when the daft old darling had locked herself out, Ralph had managed to wriggle through the narrow casement window which Annie left ajar for that extra bit of freshness. What could be wriggled in through could be wriggled out of. But Ralph was bigger and wider now. Oh what a dreadful choice: have his ankles bitten by a mutant dog and his ear wax collected and his toenails thrown into a jar in the cellar – or try that window?

He tried that window.

But not before he'd closed the toilet door.

Quick-thinking, that. Knocker could bark or scratch at a door, but he wasn't able to *open* a door. Ralph was pretty certain of that.

He stood on the seat and opened the window, punching it out until its hinges groaned, wedging it in place with its metal handle. All he had to do now was climb onto the cistern, get his body through the gap and wriggle his bum like an insane halibut. He raised his foot, just as Knocker thudded into the toilet door. So great was the throb of wood that Ralph missed his footing and almost struck his head against the window recess. He put out a hand to steady himself and managed to rip three or four sheets of newspaper off a hook on the wall. No toilet roll for the great Jack Bilt. No velvety, double-strength softness for him. Good old-fashioned, inky newsprint. Ralph scrunched it into his fist. If his fright level rose much higher than this, he could yet be needing a supply of paper.

But he made it through at the next attempt, greased by a fear that spread his tummy flatter than his mother's ironing board. He raced down the garden, past the spreading blackberry brambles and scrambled over the crumbling wall.

Sanctuary. He slid into a sitting position, put his head between his knees and breathed a huge sigh.

And there he stayed for another five minutes, until the tickle of an ant running over his hand made him open his eyes once more. He smiled at the insect, which immediately disappeared into the folds of the paper in his fist. Worried that it might become lost and squashed, Ralph opened the paper and shook the ant out. That was when he noticed the leading article. A story about a scientist gone missing. A frizzy-haired professor who, like the whistling plumber Tom Jenks, had completely and utterly vanished one day.

It could have been mere coincidence, of course, that Jack had this story on a hook in his toilet. And statistically, a one-off would have been acceptable. But the fact was this: all four sheets that Ralph was holding carried reports of the missing boffin.

Four out of four is not coincidence.

Two things were clear to Ralph from this: one, Jack Bilt was fascinated by this story; and two, he liked to wipe his bottom on it.

Grounded

'OH, LOOK AT THE STATE OF YOU.'

The words flew out of Penny's mouth like bullets. *Peeang. Pnow.* Ralph Aubrey Perfect, boy adventurer, you're dead.

'I thought you were searching for your roller blades, not digging a tunnel to the centre of the earth?'

Ralph shrugged. 'They were right in the corner,' he offered.

His mother raised a simmering eyebrow. 'You're grounded,' she said, pointing a finger. 'No skating – or tunnelling – of any kind tonight. Bath, then your room, then early to bed. No TV. No music. No complaints.'

Ralph turned away with a sullen grimace.

'And don't grimace,' said his mother.

Ralph stuck out his tongue.

And though she couldn't possibly have seen this act of cheek, Mrs Perfect added spookily, 'And don't stick your tongue out, either, young man.'

'Young man'. How Ralph hated that. He clumped upstairs, making sure he left dusty footprints everywhere, pleased to hear his mother tutting and clucking and reaching for the vacuum cleaner long before he'd started dumping clothes in the wash basket.

While he waited for the bath to fill, he sat on the bathroom floor in his dressing gown, his back against the fins of the wurgling radiator. One by one, he looked through the articles he'd snatched from the hook in Jack Bilt's loo. The first showed a photo of the missing professor, sitting in an easy chair surrounded by books. A gaunt and elderly man, he was, with deep-set, hawkish eyes and a slackness in the jaw that left his lower lip cowering away from his teeth. This is what Ralph read about him:

South Thames Police are still baffled by the mysterious disappearance of theoretical physicist Professor Ambrose Collonges (sixty-two) from his home on the outskirts of Ledlow Wood. Professor Collonges, the world's leading authority on matter to anti-matter transgeneration, was last seen by a neighbour walking his dog. Police have ruled out abduction by force, and are investigating claims that the scientist may have defected to a foreign power, taking his controversial theories with him…

Ralph raised his eyes. Transgeneration? What did that mean? He picked up the second bit of limping newsprint, holding its torn edges carefully together. It reported, roughly, the same news as the first. The third one, likewise, added little more. But the fourth made Ralph sit up with a start. Taps raged and bubble monsters foamed beside him, but he only had eyes for those columns of words. He didn't understand half the language used, but certain phrases leapt out like sparks, especially in the paragraph which explained the concept of transgeneration...

...atoms contained within a primary shell, electromagnetically stimulated by buffering radionic plexus covariants, undergo significant particle displacement activity. By selectively adjusting the bipolar energy, it is hypothetically possible, Collonges argues, to reduce or expand matter or move it through time and space in a manner roughly akin to the transporter popularised on the TV show Star Trek.

Ralph steadied his hands and read that chunk again. Particle displacement. Reduce matter. *Star Trek*.

Jack's watch.

Kyle's 'dive' into the privet hedge.

The tiny white van.

The oak tree in the bell jar.

Knocker's shrivelled leg.

Matter.

Displaced.

Ralph's eyes became a wide barometer of terror. The warmth began to drain from his tingling skin as a tidal wave of fear surged through his veins. Strangely, the sensation didn't last long as a real tidal wave of overflowing bathwater simultaneously splattered the floor by his ankle. He leapt to his feet and screwed down the taps, being careful not to get the articles wet. Only now did he realise the 'thimbleful' of bubble bath he'd thrown into the water was really more like a plant pot-ful. A huge, popping, lava bed of foam was jellying its way towards the ceiling. Leaving the articles on top of the laundry basket, he pillow-punched through it and reached for the plug. The water level gurgled down. When the tub was a sensible three-quarters full, he jammed the plug back, scraped the glistening candy-floss aside, stepped through the puddle on the floor and got in.

The overwhelming panic he'd felt had now given way to a node of deep suspicion. 'Particle displacement'. The words chimed like a bell. That was the very phrase Jack had used when Ralph had asked him about the watch. Was it possible the builder was telling the truth? Playing a wicked double bluff? That the flashing device on his bony wrist really could shrink you to the size of half a thumb – as well as display the accurate time?

Ralph dipped his head below the surface of the water and let his fringe float amongst the islands of bubbles.

Supposing it was true. Supposing Jack did have such a device. How had he obtained it? And how could a thick-sliced loaf like him be skilled enough to use it? He'd struggle to programme a video recorder, let alone work out a matter transporter. What connection could he have to the missing professor?

And then it struck him – no, not the loofah or his mum's rubber duck or the spider crawling across the ceiling high above – but a detail he'd missed in one of the reports. He dried his hands on a towel and snatched them up, finding the picture of Collonges again. The professor was sitting with his back to a window. Beyond the window was a criss-crossing pattern of dark-grey lines. They were poles. Metal scaffolding poles. Ralph put the articles aside.

The professor had been having some building work done when this photograph was taken.

That was the connection.

A bar of soap shot out of Ralph's grasp (skittling a cluster of shampoo bottles). It was clear to him now what must have happened…

One day, Jack had been up on the scaffolding, repairing a window or pointing a wall, when he'd casually peered into the professor's study and seen the old man carrying out transgeneration experiments. The builder, never slow to spot an opportunity, had eased up the window and slipped into the room. From a safe distance, he'd watched the professor displacing a pen or a paperclip or something, and evil had gripped his undernourished heart. He'd made a sound. The professor had turned, demanding to know what the devil Jack was up to. Jack had lunged and gripped him by the throat. And while the old man gurgled and his eyes began to bulge, Jack had reached for that thing he cheatingly called a watch and told the professor in acid-filled spittle that if he didn't explain how to use the gadget, he'd stretch his neck into the shape of an egg timer. The professor had nodded and Jack had eased off. But then the scientist had staggered backwards, desperately trying to destroy his equipment with huge frantic sweeps of his arm and at the same time calling to his faithful dog…Bengy. Bengy had raced in, yapping fiercely. Jack, having no other weapon to hand, had turned the transgenerator on the hound, pressing one of the pyramids at random. A radionic, bipolar, electro-magnetic discharge had beamed across the room and struck poor Bengy in his left hind leg, immediately shrinking it to the size of half a thumb!

Ralph panted hard and sat up fast, displacing more water onto the floor. He could *see it*. He could see it.

Bengy, yelping, collapsing in fear, his head turning back to his cruelly-shrivelled leg. By now, the professor would have reached his desk. He'd have a cigarette lighter in his fist, holding the flame to the brittle corners of a dog-eared manuscript; his life's work; thirty-five years of particle physics, about to transgenerate up in smoke...until Jack aims the device at him. The old man staggers back and drops his notes in panic. Jack presses the pyramid again.

At the age of sixty-two, Professor Ambrose Collonges appears to disappear, but has actually been shrunk to the size of his terrier's withered leg. And what does the builder do with him now? Does he lift up the carpet and wedge the midget genius between two floorboards? Does he feed him to the snake in the cage in the corner? Does he flick him into the upturned light shade, turn on the light and watch the miniature man frazzle?

Or does he bind him in a leaf of threadbare sandpaper, pop him in a matchbox and carry him around like some specimen, some trophy?

'Agh!' screamed Ralph as the bathroom door opened.

'Oh, stop it,' said his mother, breezing in. 'I've seen everything you've got, Ralph Perfect.' She opened the bathroom cabinet and took out a pair of nail clippers.

Nails. What if the nails in the cellar weren't Jack's?

What if he lured people into his house, shrank them and stole their fingernails?

Then removed any trace of their visit.

Ralph thought again about the van he'd found, with its miniature replica lunchbox and newspaper. If he'd checked in the back, what else would he have seen? Tools, copper piping, u-bends, taps? He looked at his mother with a face as white as the bar of soap.

'What's the matter?' she asked.

Ralph shuddered and slid down into the bath, seeking the warmth of the water on his shoulders. 'You won't believe me, Mum.'

Penny raised an eyebrow and braced herself.

'I think I know what's happened to Tom.'

Penny bakes a cake

His mother gave him the kind of look that could toast a slice of bread in three seconds flat. 'Tom?' she repeated.

Ralph thought hard. Now he was panicked. It had been, without doubt, a rash choice of words. For he had no irrefutable proof that the plumber, Tom Jenks, had been zapped by a stolen transgenerator. And how could he possibly confess to his mum that he'd sneaked into Jack's and found a tiny, white van that looked like a toy but probably belonged to the man who'd fixed their tap? How could he prove it? Even if he showed her the newspaper articles, she wouldn't be convinced about Jack's 'watch', not after the way he'd 'teased' them with it last time. Mum was as down to earth as an ant. Particle displacement? Hokum, she'd call it. Mumbo-jumbo. Claptrap. Tosh.

'Well?' she prompted. She lowered the loo seat and sat on it.

Ralph opened his mouth. He had to say something. If he couldn't tell her outright what he knew, maybe he could coax her gently towards it? 'I think he's next door,' he whispered.

Penny dropped her gaze like a car might suddenly dip its headlights. In a voice wobbling with hope she said, 'He's come back?'

'No. I don't think he ever went.'

Question marks appeared in his mother's eyes.

Ralph sponged his arm but the skin felt cold. 'I think Jack's holding him prisoner, Mum.'

'Oh, Ralph,' she tutted, sharply. 'For a moment there...'

You almost believed me, Ralph thought sadly. She wanted to, for sure. She really had liked Tom.

His mother sighed and made a show of standing up. She was halfway through the door when Ralph blurted out: 'I keep hearing noises. Scratching sounds.' He hadn't, of course, he just needed an excuse to keep her talking. Any further escapades at Number 9 would need to involve a witness, an adult. He had to keep Mum on his side.

Penny half-turned, pinching the neck of her blouse. She looked at the skirting boards and shuddered.

'It's not rats,' said Ralph, trying to reassure her. She didn't like scuttly things with tails. A mouse had pottered across the kitchen once and his mother had actually stood on a chair. 'It's like someone trying to dig. Or send us a message. Like, y'know, the Count of Crusty Minto.'

'Monte Cristo,' Penny tutted.

Near enough, Ralph thought.

But his luck was out. His mother raised her hands and flapped away the nonsense. 'Oh, this is silly. I don't even know why I'm querying this. Quite apart from the why, how could Mr Bilt have kidnapped or overpowered a man like Tom? Tom's a whacking great chap.'

Not any more, Ralph thought.

'Where would he imprison him, for goodness' sake?'

In his house, Ralph thought. The one beneath the sheeting. The one...hhh! He gasped in disbelief. The missing house. The one stolen in Yorkshire. It was here. Next door. Miniaturised by Jack.

'Besides, that policeman would have soon sniffed him out.'

Penny turned to her son and waited for an answer. 'Hello, Planet Ralph, this is 'M' calling.'

'Um?' he grunted.

'Policeman. I was saying about the policeman.'

The policeman. Ralph dropped his hands in the water, sending his submarine bobbing towards the taps. The policeman, Bone. He ought to be told. About the van. About the articles. Definitely the articles. And the house. Ralph squeezed his eyes shut and tried to picture the missing property. The paper had shown an inset of it, but that was two weeks past and Ralph couldn't remember what it had looked like, not enough to know if it matched the one in Jack's front room. There were ways to find out, though.

'Mum, after my bath, can I use the internet?'

'Ralph, which part of 'grounded' don't you understand?'

'But it's important. I want to know about that missing house in Yorkshire.'

'I'm going,' said Penny, losing patience, 'before you start to tell me Tom's been miniaturised and kept in an empty crisp packet or something.'

Ralph opened his eyes very wide.

'Ralph, that's horribly cruel,' she said. 'Even to think it. That poor man…' She shook her head, struggling to find the right words.

Ralph gave it one last throw. 'Why don't you bake him a cake?'

'Who? Bake who a cake?'

'Jack. Make a cake. We'll take it round together. You keep him talking; I'll look for Tom.'

Mrs Perfect took a slow, conversation-stopping breath. 'Ralph, will you please stop talking nonsense. This is Midfield Crescent, not a chapter from *The*

Borrowers. People stoop as they age but they do not get shrunk. Now, when you're done, it's straight to your room. Do not watch TV. Do not pass 'GO'. Do not collect any biscuits from the kitchen.'

Ralph heard and understood, but he didn't obey. He put on his dressing gown and tiptoed down the landing, passing his own room, sneaking in to Mum's. He sat on the duvet and lifted the phone from the bedside table. Quietly and accurately, he dialled seven sevens: the number of the local police station.

Almost immediately a woman's voice answered.

'Hello, could I speak to Mr Bone?' asked Ralph.

'Mr Bone?' she queried, sounding bored.

'He's a policeman.'

'We all are here,' she said. 'I think you mean Detective Inspector Bone. What's it in connection with?'

'A missing person,' Ralph said confidently.

The conversation paused. Ralph heard a brushing sound and guessed that the woman had covered the mouthpiece – but not very well, as he clearly heard her say: 'Frank, got some whispering kid on the line asking for Old Nick.'

There was muttering, then the woman said: 'Just a moment.'

And the next voice to answer was Bone's deep syrup. 'Bone,' he said bluntly.

'It's me,' said Ralph.

'And who might you be?' Bone replied impatiently.

Ralph shivered. He'd never been good with authoritative types. 'Ralph,' he said, 'the boy from Midfield Crescent. You came to my house, looking for a plumber called Tom. Have you found him?'

And he prayed the detective would say, 'Oh, yes. He'd gone to see his mother in Rhyl.' Then all fear of Jack would dissolve in an instant.

But Bone said, 'No,' in a low suspicious voice, adding, 'Why?' in an even more menacing one.

So Ralph told him about the missing professor. And how he'd 'used' the downstairs toilet at Jack's and seen all the articles and noticed the scaffolding.

Bone made a few quiet humming noises. Then he came out with something odd. 'Do you know a boy called Kyle Salter?'

'Yes,' said Ralph in a squeaky voice.

Bone sniffed. 'See much of him, do you?'

Ralph chewed his lip. 'No, not for ages.'

'Hmm.' Bone clicked his tongue. 'Only, Salter and two of his mates have done a runner. Taken off, they have, just like your plumber.'

Ralph almost dropped the phone.

'You wouldn't know anything about that, would you?'

'No,' gulped Ralph. But he did know this. The phone had just gone boomy, the way it does when someone lifts the extension. He slammed it down fast and hurtled to the bathroom. From the foot of the stairs his mother's voice shouted: 'Ralph? Were you on the phone just then?'

Ralph leapt into the bath again and prayed she wouldn't push it.

She didn't. That evening, Penny Perfect busied herself in her favourite room: the kitchen. Ralph had been in his bedroom for the best part of an hour when the scent of warm baking entered his nostrils. His twitching nose guided him onto the landing, just in time to hear the doorbell ringing.

His mother, wiping her hands on her apron, went to answer the caller. 'Oh, it's you,' Ralph heard her say. 'Would you like to step inside a moment?'

'Delighted,' said Jack, in his snake hiss of a voice.

Ralph's heart filled up with dread. He sprinted to the top of the stairs, in time to see Jack presenting his mum with a flimsy bunch of weeds. There were only three stalks and they curled over feebly. 'Picked these from the garden, my dear.'

'Oh, erm, thank you, Mr Bilt.'

'Jack,' he insisted, turning his trilby in tight little circles. On his wrist, the green light gave a wink.

'This is quite a strange coincidence,' said Penny. 'I've just, erm, finished baking you a cake.'

Jack raised an eyebrow. So did Ralph. She'd made a cake? So she was planning to go round and look at Jack's house. Yes!

Jack put a hand to his cold black heart. 'Touched. Quite moved.'

Penny grimaced and plumped her hair. 'Could I bring it round tomorrow? Say about…eleven? Perhaps we could have a coffee as well?'

'Perhaps we could share it now?' Jack said.

That had Ralph clenching his fist. He didn't like the way Jack had said that at all.

'No,' said Penny. 'Ralph has to stay at home. He's grounded tonight.'

'All the more for us without him, eh?'

'Mister Bilt!'

Jack showed her his smiling teeth. 'Popped round to ask a favour, actually.'

'Then ask,' said Penny, composing herself.

'Need a pair of rubber gloves,' the builder said

eerily. He craned his body forward, his dark eyes glinting like sugared currants. 'Big ones. I'm doing *a little experiment.*'

Elevenses With Jack

Whenever Ralph was frightened, he played football in his head. He wasn't good at football. Not on a pitch, anyway. No one ever picked him for the school eleven. Mr Carpenter said he had one right foot, one left foot and neither knew which way the other was kicking. That was why, in Games, they always put him in goal. This suited Ralph well. You didn't have to run around much in goal. You could lean against the posts in quiet moments and imagine you were holding the line for England, making breathtaking saves from Brazilian strikers who could bend a ball twice round the planet and back but still not hit the netting behind your hands. In real life, of course, it was never like that. But, boy, Ralph was good at soccer in his head.

That night, he needed to be. Never mind two, he needed to play a game of *three or four* halves to keep his pounding brain at bay. If he once stopped tipping shots over the crossbar or parrying headers away at close range his brain would start to boil like a pan of soup. Glop. Glop. Bubble. Gloop. Then egg-shaped swellings would erupt in his skull as hideous notions popped into his head, each more gigantic, more fantastic than the last. Each involving a pair of rubber gloves.

What could Jack want with a pair or rubber gloves?

Mum had loaned him her very best pair. They were cherry red, oversized and reached way up her forearms. They had double-thick padding and the finger ends were bloated. They made Mum look like a circus clown.

They made Jack's eyes pop out on stalks.

'Ideal,' he'd called them. 'Just the ticket.'

That was the moment the footy kicked off inside Ralph's head. A game of frantic, all-night action. But in the pauses, the set plays, the corner kicks, the rebounds, the time spent waiting for the crowd to return the ball into play, his mind began to conjure up dastardly experiments. *Little* experiments. Involving *electricity*. For outside, rain was slapping the windows. And every now and then, a fork of lightning would bleach the curtains and tangle with the shadows. In these brief high-voltage moments, Ralph's mind would pitch into the room next door. And there would be Jack, hunched over his fish tank and shrunken house, haloed by a grisly pale-blue light, wielding a pair of smoke-charred electrodes joined to a lightning rod on his dog-servant's collar by wires fat with the zing of current. And all that was saving him from crackling like pork were Mum's rubber gloves…rubber gloves…rubber gloves…

'Hey you, wake up.'

'No, don't fry the ants!' Ralph screamed. His bedroom swam into focus. His poster of Batman. His computer, blinking. His clothes lying in a heap on his chair. His mum with a vacuous look on her face. Everything normal. Phew.

'I was thinking of boiling them for a change,' she said. 'Up. Get. Now, please.' She dangled a smelly sock over his nose.

Old socks. Vomarama. Always did the trick. Ralph sprang up like a rifle target. 'What time is it?'

'Daytime,' his mother said dryly. She threw a fresh sweatshirt at him. 'Wear this. We're going visiting, remember?'

A quick dream fragment scorched Ralph's mind: Jack grinning, wild with laughter, wringing his rubber-gloved hands as he approached…

'No, Mum. We can't. It's a trap. We mustn't go.'

His mother tossed a pair of jeans onto the bed. 'I baked a cake,' she said. End of argument.

It was an apricot-jam sponge. A triple-decker special. The top was garnished with real fruit slices and mouth-watering dollops of freshly-whipped cream. The very second Ralph saw it, he wanted to beat his boyish chest and become a Neanderthal gateau hunter. He could wrestle alligators for that cake. Overturn dinosaurs. Hand-fight orcs. That cake had to feel the clamp of his teeth. Forget Jack, that cake was *his*.

'Hands off,' said his mum, tapping his wrist. They were standing at the door to Number 9 and Ralph had just reached for a squirt of butter filling, bulging seductively from the middle and upper layers.

'Can't I just—?'

'No. You don't touch this cake. Not even if Mr Bilt wants to share it.'

No cake? Ralph was taken aback. His mum had never engaged in gastronomic torture before. Why start now?

The door to the house swung open. Jack, dressed in a moth-eaten pin-striped suit, stood to attention when he saw the gift.

'Exquisite,' he whispered.

And Knocker agreed. The little terrier begged and tried to sit up. But that cruel combination of intense nasal twitching and lack of a good leg made him topple over with an awkward bump.

'Come in,' Jack said, coughing a cloud of smoke from his lungs. He stubbed his cigarette out on the step, then yanked Penny down the hall.

Ralph closed the door behind them. He looked down at Knocker, who was whimpering pathetically and licking his stick. 'Bengy?' he whispered. The dog didn't respond. 'Bruce?' Ralph tried. 'Pongo? Monty? Rover?'

'Knocker,' Jack roared from within the front room. 'Git in here, now.'

Knocker pricked his ears. Down the hall he knocked.

So that was his name, then: Knocker. Poor mutt.

The 'lounge' was little changed from the last time Ralph had been here. Jack hadn't made any effort to tidy. Apart from the sofa, all available surfaces were gridlocked with mugs or unwashed dinner plates. Papers flew amok. Tools were scattered carelessly about. If anything, there was more mess now than before, especially around the wardrobe cabinet, where bits of curly wire and some scraps of twisted metal were littering the floor. Jack had done some work on it. There was now a long mirror on the back wall of the cabinet and two narrow sets of vertical tracks, running down the insides from top to bottom. Around head height (Jack's head height), two three-pronged forks of thin sheet-metal poked out into the room like misshapen, old-fashioned railway signals. They were attached to a pair of trolley wheels and were clearly meant to roll up and down the tracks. But why? To what immoral end?

Amazingly, Penny beat Ralph to the question. Nodding at the cabinet she said, 'My goodness, what on earth is that?'

Ralph quickly scanned its base for the van. Drat. It wasn't there. He took a sideways glance at the trestle table, too. But the fish tank was covered and it was still too early for an 'innocent' inquiry about what lay beneath the plastic sheet.

Jack laced his fingers under his chin and put himself between the cabinet and Penny. 'Later,' he said, with excruciating sleaze. 'Cosy yourself. Take a seat, do.'

Penny looked at the sofa and swallowed.

'Allow me,' said Jack. He brushed away a heap of blackened matchsticks, then beat the sagging cushions half-dead, spraying brick dust and fag ash into the air. He robbed a Sunday paper of its *Home and Garden* supplement and spread a few sheets out over the seats.

They crumpled and tore as Penny sat down. 'Thank you. Erm, where shall I put the cake?'

'On the floor,' said Jack, 'anywhere you like.'

Penny glanced at the slavering Knocker.

Jack reached down and shut the dog's mouth. 'Wouldn't touch it. Trained to perfection.'

Unconvinced, Penny put the cake by her ankles. 'But

you'll have a piece, won't you, Mr Bilt? I hope you like sherry. I, erm, dashed a little into the mix.'

Strange, thought Ralph. She sounds as though she's begging him. In his experience, no one had ever needed to be begged before to taste his mother's cooking.

Jack's tongue did an ugly circuit of his lips. 'Coffee,' he suggested. 'Lubricates the crumbs.' He spat into the watering can beside Knocker's bowl. To Ralph's disgust, the terrier knocked up and licked the rose.

Jack clinked three mugs against Ralph's chest. 'Wash these,' he said. 'Coffee's on the fridge.'

Ralph looked at his mum. She gave a frugal nod. 'Bring plates as well – and a big knife, Ralphy.'

Jack slanted his eyes.

'For the cake, Mr Bilt.'

With a hand across his midriff, he bowed to her.

Ralph took the mugs into the kitchen. The place was revolting; a playground for bacteria. On every single plate crammed into the sink there were hardened remains of corned beef, new potatoes and fruity brown sauce. Some lifestyle. Some diet. Was that all Jack ate? Corned beef, potatoes and the odd bowl of porridge? He moved the mixer tap to a crockery-free zone, filled the kettle and washed the mugs.

He turned to the fridge. The coffee wasn't there.

O-kaaay, that meant he could search the cupboards. He did so. Quickly. All of them, bar one (a canned food hoard), were Mother Hubbard bare.

The kettle clicked off. Ralph thought again. He hadn't looked in the fridge itself. He yanked the door open. The foil top jiggled off a half-empty milk bottle. Ralph reached in, intending to take it, but found his eye drawn to an object on the central shelf. It was the box Jack had carried under his arm when he'd first arrived to look at Annie's house, the day the Salter gang had been dispensed with.

Ralph felt his heart begin a deep *pump, pump*. He took the box out. It was fixed by a single clasp, nothing more. Trembling, he crouched down and opened it. A luminescent, pale-green light immediately began to radiate forth. Ralph dropped the lid fast and pushed the box further into the fridge before opening it again, very, very carefully. The green light bounced around the shiny white surfaces, fogging the clouds of his cooling breath. Its source, he could see now, was some kind of stone, pulsing with an energy from deep within.

Dare he touch it?

He shut the box.

He opened it again.

His eyes shone green.

His heart *pump, pumped.*

He shut the box again.

He opened it wide.

His heart *pump, pumped.*

He took the stone.

He wrapped it in a tissue and put it in his pocket, then closed the fridge door and stood up quickly.

Knocker was sitting in the doorway, watching.

Ralph fell back against the window in fear.

But the dog did not alert its master. Something clearly wasn't right with the mutt. His eyelids had settled to halfway open and he was swaying gently, even though he was sitting. For one moment, Ralph wondered about the stone. Could it be controlling Knocker? Or making him sick, like kryptonite did to Superman? Ralph turned his pocket towards the dog. Knocker seemed no worse for the movement. But he grizzled and slavered and that gave him away: there were greasy smears of butter filling all around his jowls.

'The cake,' Ralph whispered. 'You've eaten the cake.'

The cake, the whole cake and nothing but the cake.

Knocker raised his stick and promptly broke wind, then stagger-knocked back to the lounge again.

Ralph followed, pinching his nose. Just as he suspected, the cake plate was clean.

Amazingly, his mother hadn't seen it. She was peering at Jack and he was peering at her. 'Small confession to make,' he was saying, mincing his hands in his mesmerising way.

Ralph gulped and touched the stone in his pocket. He didn't know why, but he felt comforted by it.

Knocker trumped again and rolled onto his back with his three good legs and his stick in the air.

'Confession?' said Penny.

'Tiny secret,' said Jack. He held up the rubber gloves and flapped them limply. 'Not really a builder,' he said.

The End of the Pier Show

'INVENTOR?' The word screeched like a missile from the back of Ralph's throat, echoing Jack's supposed 'confession'.

'Ralph,' said his mum, in one of those 'we're in company, *remember*?' voices.

Ralph jutted a finger. 'But he's not an *inventor*, Mum. He's—'

'Ralph!' she snapped, making Knocker bark drunkenly. Ralph glanced at the dog. He was blotto. Plastered. Just how much sherry had Mum put in that cake – that cake she was desperate for Jack to try? He bit his tongue. Now wasn't the time to ask. When his mother's tone sharpened up like this, it was possible to understand how a joint of meat felt when she drove a long metal skewer through it. Besides, he wanted to hear Jack's tale.

'Inventor?' Penny repeated.

'Cherished childhood ambition,' said Jack. 'Been a builder. Messy. Didn't take to it much.'

'Then you're not doing up the house?'

Jack creased his nose. 'Needed a workshop, somewhere quiet.'

Penny nodded and let her gaze rove. She winced at the sight of a dead mouse in the corner. 'And what do you invent, exactly?'

Good question, thought Ralph. Go for it, Mum. It's obvious he's lying. Toothpaste him. Squeeze the truth out of him. Now.

Jack flippered the rubber gloves together. A glint lit the centres of his quick, grey eyes. 'Attractions,' he said. 'Slot machines. Novelties.'

Ralph gave a snort of contempt. 'Prove it,' he said, inviting yet another scowl from his mother. He didn't care. She'd be grateful to him later. Jack Bilt was lying through his tar-stained teeth.

Jack, who'd been crouching like an eager slip-fielder, snapped his shoulders back and said, 'A demonstration, I think.'

He marched to the wardrobe. Before Ralph or his mum could say another word, he had fitted the gloves over the protruding metal prongs so that they resembled a grotesque pair of hands. He flicked a switch somewhere. The cabinet lights began to pulse. He turned to Penny. 'You or the boy?'

'No,' cried Ralph. 'He's going to miniaturise you, Mum!'

'Oh, Ralph,' she tutted, 'just be quiet a second, will

you?' She looked steadily at Jack. 'What is that device?'

'I call it...*The Frisker*,' Jack said proudly. 'A curiosity. A jest. A quite...*shocking* experience.'

Penny stood up.

Ralph gasped. 'Mum, no!'

She took his hand off her arm and tapped his wrist.

'Step up,' said Jack, 'for the End of the Pier Show.'

Penny touched her lip. 'Are you saying that you're building a series of amusements? For a seaside arcade of some kind?'

'In one,' Jack said. 'Roll up, do.' He curled an inviting hand.

Penny approached the lights, stopping between the outstretched gloves.

Now Ralph was desperate. But what could he do? If he spoke about the van or the house or the cellar then Jack would know he'd been snooping around. But if he didn't...

'Which way do I face?' asked Penny.

'Into the mirror,' Jack said wormily.

'No,' cried Ralph and thrust a hand into his pocket, intending to bring out the stone he'd found in the box in the fridge. It was his only hope, he thought. Distract Jack and make him spill the truth. But he hit the wrong pocket, and by the time his mistake had been realised, Jack had set *The Frisker* in motion.

With a *whup, whup, whup,* the rubber hands clapped down over Penny's body, from her shoulders to her hips to her ankles and back again.

She wriggled.

She giggled.

But she didn't disappear.

The motor died. The red gloves shuddered to a rubbery stop. 'You are clean,' a tinny voice squeaked from a small speaker grille on the front of the device. 'No bulges. No hidden weapons.'

Penny patted her tummy, blew a kiss curl and smiled. 'I don't know about bulges,' she said.

'Again?' asked Jack, and hit the switch anyway.

Whup. Whup. Whup. Off the hands went.

Penny Perfect squealed like a dizzy schoolgirl.

Ralph couldn't believe it. Total embarrassment. He laid his fists by his sides in disgust. Mum was actually *enjoying* this. She'd always liked fairgrounds and magic shows and stuff, but what had happened to her desire to find Tom? Someone had to force the issue here. Someone *sensible*. Someone who *knew* the terrible truth. 'What's that, under there?' He pointed at the trestle table.

Jack's eyes tapered down to slits. 'None of your bloomin' business,' he hissed. He switched off *The Frisker*. 'Cake?' he asked Penny.

'Knocker's scoffed it,' said Ralph.

'All of it?!' Penny whirled round and gaped at the empty plate.

'Git up,' snarled Jack, giving the dog a toe poke in the ribs.

Knocker scrabbled to his feet, bumping one leg of the trestle table and rocking its cargo back and forth. Jack lunged forward and threw his arms around it, catching it before it could topple to the ground. The stolen transgenerator blinked on his wrist, its green light matching the stone in Ralph's pocket.

'Show us what's under the sheet,' he said.

'Where's the coffee?' Jack growled.

'Where's Tom?' Ralph hit back, bold as you like. He was feeling strangely confident now. He felt sure that the stone he'd found in the fridge was connected with the workings of the particle displacer. He had that stone. And Jack didn't know it.

'Tom?' Jack's mouth curled into a sneer.

'Mr Jenks,' said Penny, parting her lips with a nervous tongue. 'The plumber who came here to quote for a job.'

Jack raised his chin. 'What's Jenks to you?'

'Nothing,' said Penny, picking her nails. 'Nothing at all. It's just...he was going to do some work on our house as well and, erm, you were one of the last people to see him. We were wondering if you could throw any light on his disappearance?'

Jack's eyes came even closer together. 'Like him, don't you?' he said very coldly, as Knocker grizzled and tottered around the floor. With great comic timing, he stumbled forward and fell through the gaping hole in the boards. A small hill of dust puffed out of the gap.

Penny saw it as a chance to escape Jack's glare. 'Oh dear. Poor Knocker. We'd better—'

'Leave him,' said Jack. He moved towards the table. 'Boy wants to see the main attraction. Let's show him.' He whipped the blue sheet back over his shoulder.

There, on the table, was the large, long fish tank; four walls of glass with an open top. Penny stooped down and peered through the glass. 'Oh, a house. How... unusual.'

'Miniville,' said Jack. 'Prize exhibit.'

Ralph stepped forward for a closer look. But the house just swam in front of his eyes as his mind began to connect the name Miniville to all his darkest theories and fears.

'Did you build it?' asked Penny.

'I'm the landlord,' said Jack.

That means he's got lodgers, Ralph thought dizzily. And he knew he should have warned his mother what this meant. But his normally dependable twelve-year-old brain had been completely unhinged by a line from his favourite repeat TV show, a series called *Lost in Space*, in which a robot was often heard to cry '*Danger!*' to a boy called Will Robinson.

Danger, Ralph Perfect!

Danger! Danger!

Ralph was just too scared to speak.

Penny knitted her eyebrows, worried by Jack Bilt's overbearing smugness. 'It looks so real. Why are you keeping it inside a fish tank?'

'Because there's no escape,' said Jack.

And that was the vital prod Ralph needed, to get his stuck tongue working again. 'Mum,' he panted, 'the house *is* real. It's the one that went missing on the Yorkshire Moors. He stole it. Just like he stole the machine that shrank it.'

Penny shook her head and looked quizzically at Jack.

'Boy's right,' he said. 'Should have called him Sherlock. I'm a rogue. I'm a rascal. A rozzer's dodger. They should lock me up, they should.'

'What's going on here?' Penny said soberly. Her

accommodating smiles had all been put away. She wasn't going to tolerate any more nonsense. When Jack didn't answer, she took Ralph's arm. 'That's it. We're leaving. Come on, Ralph.'

Jack stepped sideways and blocked her path. 'Very neat. Both together. I could almost say *perfect*.' He drew back his sleeve. The transgenerator pulsed.

'Stand aside,' said Penny.

'I think not,' said Jack. He turned the red pyramid on his wrist.

Ralph felt as though his guts had been put into a bag, spin-dried and hit with a very large hammer. In a flash, the world disappeared to a point, like the last lick of ice cream in the bottom of a cone. There was a sudden rush of light, then darkness, then cold. He came to with a painful jolt, finding himself on a wooden floor that smelt of damp and long neglect. His mother was on her knees beside him.

'I feel sick. What happened?' She clutched at her stomach.

Then a voice said, 'No, not you as well.'

Ralph and his mother looked over their shoulders. A tall figure in blue came hurrying towards them.

It was the long-lost plumber, Tom Jenks.

It's a Small World

Penny stood up slowly, crossing her arms like a mummified pharaoh. 'Where are we?' she whispered, in a voice filled with confusion and fear.

Tom moved forward and held her by the shoulders. 'You're in Miniville,' he said, as calmly as he could. 'You're in the parlour at the front of the house Jack's…renovating.'

Penny backed away, shaking her head. She looked around at the bare grey walls; at the threadbare rug, too ditched and dirty to reveal any pattern; at the broken pelmets above the high stately windows, once sturdy enough to take four or five metres of heavy drapes; at the huge stone fireplace, sooted and dead; at the ceiling rose and its unlit chandelier; and then again at Tom: sympathetic, kind, but utterly helpless.

'It is me,' he whispered, 'underneath all this.' He ran his hands around twenty days of stubble. 'I'm afraid you've been miniaturised, just like the rest of us.'

Penny lurched forward, trying not to vomit.

'It's OK,' Tom said, not letting her fall. 'Breathe slowly and deeply. The dizziness soon passes.'

'Ralph?' she gasped, struggling to look for him.

'I'm here, Mum,' he said. He was over by a tall bay window, looking out. Beyond its broken panes of glass, through the wall of the 'aquarium' in which the house sat, he could see Jack's monstrous, gloating face, distorted like a curved reflection in a door knob. In a rolling thunder that shook the light fittings, the house shuddered and rocked to the builder's laughter.

He had them.

Ralph and Penny.

Miniones.

'Let us out!' cried Ralph. He beat a loose pane, causing it to crash into jags at his feet.

His mother squealed and covered her ears.

'It's no good, Ralph,' said Tom, calming Penny again. 'You're too small; he can't hear you. Don't give him the satisfaction of seeing you upset.'

'But we can escape. I can climb through this window.'

'Yes, and you can walk out of the front door any time you like. But you won't get over the walls of the tank. They're too high and too smooth. Trust me, we've tried.'

'We?' Ralph said. The sound of hurrying feet made him turn towards the door. Three more mini-people burst into the parlour: a middle-aged man with thick, black glasses and a ginger beard, wearing a pale-brown carpenter's apron; a much younger, spiky-haired fellow in tracksuit bottoms and a plaster-splattered sweatshirt; and behind them, catching up fast...Kyle Salter!

'You,' Kyle spat.

'You,' Ralph echoed. He sounded flippant, but he didn't mean to be. In truth, he was dreadfully scared. He'd suspected all along that Kyle's disappearance was connected with Jack. And here was the living proof – in miniature. All the things he'd imagined were coming true. It was a horrible, dark, unsettling feeling.

'You caused this, didn't you?' Kyle said, and charged towards Ralph as if he, and he alone, were responsible for their entire predicament.

'Hey,' Tom shouted, catching Kyle's arm and spinning him off-balance. 'That's enough of that. We're all in this together. You know the rules. No in-fighting.'

'He's a nerd,' Kyle said. 'I *knew* he'd turn up.'

'Yeah, it's a small world, Kyle. Now behave.' Tom pushed him back towards the grim-faced carpenter, who spoke in a softened Yorkshire accent.

'We heard t'glass breaking. Wondered what were up?'

'New arrivals,' said Tom.

The carpenter tugged his beard. 'They'll not be labourers, surely?'

'Please,' implored Penny, fingers fluttering against her

temples, 'will someone explain to me *what* is going on?'

Tom guided her away from the window, away from the cartoon figure of Jack. The builder was watching through a magnifying glass. A *magnifying* glass. Ralph kicked himself, remembering how he'd seen it sitting by the fish tank. All the clues were there, all along.

'Come upstairs,' Tom said quietly to Penny. 'It's warmer. There's food. We'll explain the whole story, when you've met the others.'

'How many people has he captured?' gulped Ralph.

'Thirteen, with you two,' the plasterer said, just as a dreadful moaning sound came floating through the air like a fire alarm siren.

'Duck!' Tom shouted, forcing Penny down.

The carpenter quickly grabbed hold of Ralph's collar and almost dragged him into the fireplace. A millisecond later, a small section of metal piping flew across the room and smashed into the wall behind Ralph's head, making a clank that rang throughout the house.

'Correction: fourteen,' the plasterer said.

Ralph looked in the direction from which the piping had come. There was no one there.

'That were Miriam,' said the carpenter.

'Our ghost,' said Kyle.

Ralph shuddered, remembering the house was haunted. 'M-Miriam?' he said.

Tom nodded, tight-lipped. 'Another minor complication. Watch out for her. She likes to throw things about. She's what you might call a 'restless spirit'.'

With that, he led them out of the parlour through a bleak, grey hall and onto the sweep of a winding staircase. At the foot of the stairs, a dumpy little man in grubby, white overalls was staring doggedly up at the wall.

'How's it going?' Tom asked.

'Champion,' said the man, watching with pride as a strip of paper peeled neatly off the wall and hung in place like a scroll of butter. 'Had to water the paste mix down a touch. Cracked it now, though. Breath of wind touches the seam, it peels.'

'Well done,' said Tom, giving him a pat.

Well done? thought Ralph. He'd never seen such a useless decorator; the bloke couldn't make a postage stamp stick.

He was about to say something about it when Tom clamped a hand against his shoulder and said, 'Careful where you're putting your feet.' He diverted Ralph from a jagged hole in a loosely-tacked step. Puzzled, Ralph altered course. The stairs were terrible, worse than the wallpaper. There were dents and holes and cracks all over. Insects were boring into the handrail. Every step squeaked or dipped or groaned. Ralph stood on one board that creaked so much he thought his knee joints had prised apart. This was weird. Peeling paper. Creaking boards. He looked at the tools on the carpenter's belt and saw hammers and a saw and a bag of old nails. He couldn't help but ask, 'You're a carpenter, aren't you? Can't you make the stairs a bit safer?'

A red flush grew under the ginger beard. 'Neville Gibbons,' said the man, shaking Ralph's hand. 'Thirty-seven years' experience in wood. Never thought I'd have to do a job like this.' He dug a dagger-shaped splinter out of a step. 'I'm not s'posed to *improve* t'stairs, lad. I'm s'posed to make 'em wonky as jelly. Just like Tom makes t'plumbing buggle, and Wally here – our plasterer and electrician – makes all t'lighting flicker. Sam, who you just saw larruping paste, has to make sure t'paper only half sticks agen' the walls.'

'But why?' asked Ralph, as they stepped onto a landing about as straight as a pasta twist. Feeling giddy, he grabbed for the banister. It broke in his hands, sending him windmilling towards the stairwell.

Once again, his shirt collar acted as his saviour. Only

this time, his rescuer was Kyle Salter. 'You can't trust nothing in Miniville,' said Kyle. 'Everything here is topsy-turvy, *rearranged*, just like your face is gonna be when we get out of here.' He glowered at Tom, then pulled Ralph to safety.

'We'll explain when you're settled,' Tom said, relieved. 'Kyle's right, though. You have to be careful here. The place is ramshackle, falling apart. Nothing is quite what it seems. Come on.'

Again he led them on, down a maze of corridors that dipped first one way, then the other. To either side, they passed rooms with little or no furnishings: a broken chair here, a leaning wardrobe there. In one room stood an old Victorian bath, with a tap that appeared to be dripping blood. Ralph was relieved to see another decorator pop up behind it, wielding a brush and a tin of red paint. What *was* going on here? He caught up with Tom and was about to pose the question when he heard a spooky rattle of chains. He stopped with a jolt. Tom and the others, too.

'What was that?' asked Penny, lifting her gaze.

The rattle came again, followed by the transiting thud of feet across a ceiling that barely seemed able to support them. Then a wail broke out and a man's voice cried: 'Melt the heater!'

Or something like it. That was the best fit Ralph could manage. The voice was far away and woefully distressed. 'Is that another g-ghost?' he asked.

'We're not sure,' said Tom, drawing them further down the corridor, until they paused beside a rounded wall. In the centre of the wall was a heavy wooden door. It was smaller than average and arched at its peak. Arm-width bands of rusting metal, each with an iron stud at their centre, criss-crossed over its four main panels. Ralph took it as a sign that he shouldn't enter and was quietly relieved when Tom said, 'It's locked. We don't have a key. It leads to the tower room, we think. At night, from outside, we can see a candle burning. So there's definitely someone – or something – in there. Mrs Spink, one of the people you'll meet in a minute, thinks it might be Miriam's 'partner'. She has what she calls 'psychic intuitions'.'

Penny shuddered. The movement kept a small amount of colour in her face.

'I reckon it's a madman,' Kyle muttered, narrowing his eyes as the manic screech of a madman's laughter seeped through the door and jangled their bones.

'Pelt the preacher!' the crazed voice moaned.

Or something close that rhymed with that. Ralph couldn't guess and he didn't want to think. He didn't like this place. If his guts weren't happily twisting with terror, his brain was kicking his stomach into touch. He slumped against the far wall, dizzy with fright, suffering the instantaneous nausea that only a certain kind of dread can bring: the fear of the imagined, the nameless unknown. Darkness swept over him like a cloak. Within five seconds, the surge of panic had become too much, and before Tom could steady him, he'd completely blacked out.

About Miniville

When he came to, he was lying on a mattress underneath a pair of rough cotton sheets. At least, that's what it felt like at first. A quick dig revealed that the 'sheets' were actually tissue paper and the 'mattress' was one of the sponge-backed scouring pads Jack had cadged out of Penny's kitchen cupboards, both shrunk down to a size appropriate for mini-people to sleep on. Looking round, Ralph could see lots of other mini 'beds', laid out like graves around the walls of the room. It reminded him of scout camp – the horror film version. Welcome to Miniville, Master Perfect.

He was in a high-ceilinged, rectangular room. Directly above him, a broken chandelier hung down at an angle from a plaster rose. It was cold and the air was ugly with damp. The tall balcony windows were closed, but a draught from a broken pane was clashing with the flames of a small log fire, burning smokily in the large Gothic fireplace. Several miniones were hunkering in front of it, including Tom, Neville and Penny. Ralph sat upright, preparing to call to them, when a younger figure stepped in front of him.

'Fancy a bite to eat, *Rafe?*' It was Kyle Salter. He broke what looked like the shell of a candy sweet and skimmed it into the middle of Ralph's chest. 'Get used to it, *old bean*. Menu's kind of limited.'

Ralph let it bounce and refused to pick it up. He hated being picked on, and he hated it even more when people made fun of any part of his name. The first day he'd met young Kyle Howard Salter, the bully had said, 'Your name's *Perfect?* Well get you, snooty.' And that was bad enough. But when Kyle had then found out that 'Rafe' (pronounced to rhyme with 'waif') was a trendy contraction of 'Ralph', he'd teased and jeered and never stopped saying it. Ralph could have happily put a fist in Kyle's mouth. But where would that have got him? In hospital, not Miniville.

'Mum,' he shouted.

Penny hurried over. 'Are you OK? Are you OK?' She kissed his head, loudly.

'Pathetic,' Kyle muttered, and walked away laughing.

Ralph stood up, candy shell breaking underfoot. As it happened, he *did* feel dreadfully hungry and was about to ask his mum if there was anything to eat when he saw, in one corner, what he thought at first was a stack of small gas cylinders. They were multicoloured and ranging in size from torpedo-shaped to large round footballs. It was only when Kyle took a stick to one and cracked off a lump and started to eat it that Ralph twigged what the objects really were: not cylinders, but sugar beads – from Mum's loaned tub of hundreds and thousands.

Food for the fishes. It made him want to yak.

'Everyone,' said Tom, calling for attention. 'This is Ralph, Penny's son. They came from next door.'

Ralph shuddered and suddenly felt weak behind his knees. He didn't like the tense that Tom had used: *came* from next door. Were they destined to stay here in Miniville for ever?

People muttered their 'hellos' or offered their sympathies. Most were workmen of one kind or another. As well as Tom, Neville and Wally – plumber, carpenter, electrician – there was a stocky Irish roofer called Spud O'Hare; a green-wellied gardener called Mrs Spink, who for some reason stood twice as tall and twice as skinny as the rest of the captives; and a well-spoken architect named Rodney Coiffure. And beside the fire, looking as if she'd cried all of Cinderella's tears, was a ragged, grim-faced Jemima Culvery, the only girl in the Salter gang. She scowled at Ralph, then returned her stare to the crackling fire, as if she'd like to be the next log on it.

Tom gave Ralph a drink of water in a can. 'No mugs,'

he explained. 'We have to make do with what we can find and what Jack chooses to send our way. It's a pretty miserable existence, I'm afraid.' He crouched in front of Penny, who was holding Ralph's hand. 'We've got lighting and some running water; Jack miniaturised in a generator and pump, but they're for the house use, not for us. In the room next door there's an old, cracked sink I plumbed into the system. You can wash in it but I wouldn't advise drinking from the taps; Jack made me fur them up with algae.'

Ralph grimaced and pulled his mouth back from his can. 'Why is everything so disgusting?'

'I'll explain in a minute,' Tom replied. 'The water you're drinking is clean, we think. There's a barrel over there in the corner by the door. Two tins per day, no more. That's the rule. Fresh water is precious here.'

'How do you get it?' asked Penny.

'You'll see,' Kyle sniffed.

Tom ignored him and said, 'There are no showers or baths. It's a standing agreement that we don't swap complaints about body odour. We all accept we stink like polecats.'

Penny blushed and looked away.

'There's a toilet facility on the ground floor. It flushes – just – if you pull the chain hard. The waste goes into a septic tank that Neville and I dug in the shallow strip of earth around the outside of the house. It's makeshift and not at all pleasant. We keep it clean so the flies don't come.'

'Flies?' Ralph took a gulp of air.

'Big furry buzzy things,' Kyle said (buzzing). 'Any good with a spear, *Rafe?*' He pointed to a cluster of sharpened stakes, stacked beside a bundle of home-made torches. Ralph took a shaky sip of water. Flies? They'd be half the size of Tom.

'You're free to sleep where you like,' Tom said, 'but so far we've all stayed together for support. As you can see, the bedding's not ideal. If you have trouble sleeping, there are one or two tasselled cushions lying about. They're as old and dusty as the house itself, but a little more comfortable than the cotton wool bud-tips Jack expects us to lay our weary heads on.'

Penny forced her fingers through her curly brown hair, clipping it back above the level of her ears. 'Why's he *doing* this? Why is Jack keeping you here?'

'We're his workforce,' said Neville.

'His *miniones*,' said Ralph.

'He must have bragged to you about his inventions?' said Wally, rubbing at the smoke burns on his face. Ralph wondered with a gulp just how 'bad' Wally had to be at his job. Judging by the spikes in his short, blond hair he'd suffered an electrical shock or two. He offered Penny a piece of sugar bead.

She smiled and shook her head. 'He said something about this house being his 'prize exhibit'.'

'It's the feature of his seaside show,' said Tom. 'It's the house we talked about that morning in your kitchen, the one that went missing from the Yorkshire Dales. He didn't take it apart; he shrank it down so he could put it on display on the end of a pier.'

Penny shook her head. 'That doesn't make sense. When people see it they'll recognise it, won't they?'

'Not if their minds can't believe it,' said Tom. 'He wants Wally to wire up a sign above the door: MINIVILLE: THE TINY HOUSE OF HORROR.'

Penny shuddered and clutched at her arms.

Tom reached forward and boldly touched her hand. Ralph watched his mum's thumb curl over the plumber's work-hardened fingers and was glad she had someone strong to protect her. 'Before he miniaturised me,' Tom said quietly, 'he told me how Miniville's supposed to work. When we've finished building, he plans to set the house inside a sealed glass dome, a bit like a giant snow-shaker.'

'And shake us up and down?' Ralph reeled in terror.

He didn't fancy being a squash ball against these ceilings.

'Rafe, shut up and listen,' Kyle snarled, whittling away at the end of a spear.

Tom went on, 'In the glass around the dome, he's going to install a number of prisms. The idea's pretty basic: when you put your eye to one, you'll see a distorted view of the house – the corner of a room, a seat-cushion, the bath. There'll be hearing points, too. And smelling holes, we think.'

'To what end?' asked Penny, looping her hair.

Neville stepped forward, puffing at a pipe. 'Greed, Mrs Perfect: Jack reckons folks'll pay a pretty penny to watch th'antics of t'Miniville ghosts.'

On cue in the distance, the crazed voice shouted, 'Help the teacher!' (or something like that). Miriam wailed an angry response. The resulting blast of air blew out Neville's pipe and bounced the door right back against the wall, springing a screw from its straining hinges.

Penny and Ralph both yelped in shock. But as the door knob dropped off and rolled down the landing, Tom merely said, 'You've done well there, Nev.'

'Aye,' Neville said, relighting his pipe. 'Just a matter of adjusting tension in t'hinges.'

'Done well?' Ralph queried. The door was hanging like a broken wing.

Tom laughed, a welcome relief in the gloom. 'You haven't quite got it yet, have you, Ralph? Jack's not using us to do the house up; it's the opposite he wants: for us to do the house *down*. He's using expert craftsmen – and women – to make stairs creak and have lights flicker—'

'And curtains billow,' Mrs Spink chipped in, going past with a length of neatly-ripped voile.

'—he wants the place to look and sound as spooky as possible. We're creating—'

'*Noah's Ark,*' muttered Penny.

Several people looked her way.

Neville moved a pencil stub from one ear to the other.

'I know what Mum means,' said Ralph. 'When I was eight, we went on holiday to Blackpool. There was this boat near the pier called *Noah's Ark*. When you walked through it, weird things happened: skulls appeared, or air would blow up your trouser leg, or you'd go through a hall of mirrors or something.'

'Like a ghost train,' Jemima muttered.

'Yes,' Ralph said. This house was like a living ghost train.

Penny looked around the room, at the mouse holes in the skirtings and the black mould peppering the ageing walls. 'And when you've finished 'building', what happens then?' She checked the faces. All were blank.

'We're not sure,' said Tom. 'We're hoping – praying – he'll let us go.'

Kyle snorted and flopped out onto a mattress. 'He's a loony,' he muttered. 'He'll never let us go.'

'Not with an attitude like that,' Tom said. 'If we work together, we *will* get out.'

'Sure. And when we do, we'll be dog meat. *Magic.*'

Ralph looked anxiously at Tom and Neville.

'Best tell him,' said Neville.

Tom rubbed his brow.

This is bad, thought Ralph. *Even Tom's scared.* Helplessness gripped him as the plumber explained: 'The device Jack uses to miniaturise things keeps a record in a binary database. It logs the coordinates of each object shrivelled.'

'You mean he always knows where we are?' asked Penny.

'Worse than that,' said Kyle. 'The devil dog's got a tracker on its collar. If we run and Jack lets Knocker come after us, *schlup*—'

'Don't,' said Jemima, pressing her fists to her ears. 'I

don't want to hear this.' A tear streaked down the valley of her nose. Penny went across and put an arm around her. 'I want my mum,' Jemima sobbed.

'We all do,' said Kyle, and in his eyes Ralph could see that the bully truly meant it.

'What happens if you don't do the work?' he asked.

Kyle drew a breath as sharp as a spear point. He pointed to a tall blue vase on the mantelpiece. At first glance, it looked like an ordinary piece of pottery, but when Ralph squinted closely he could see a boy's face mixed up in the glaze. It was Luke Baker, one of the gang.

'Luke wouldn't do what he was told,' said Kyle, 'so Jack mixed him up with the particles of the pot. And when Sylvia tried to stand up for him...' he cocked his head at Mrs Spink, '...he stretched her out like chewing gum. He can do anything with that thing: shrink you, move you, take you apart.'

'That's how you got into the hedge,' Ralph muttered, remembering back to Jack's clash with the gang. 'He 'beamed' you into it, like on *Star Trek*.'

'Yeah, thanks for reminding me, Rafe, *old chap*.'

'Oh, will you leave him alone?' Penny growled.

Salter just laughed and clicked his tongue.

Ralph shied away, anxious and hurt. The prospect of

spending the rest of his life on the bully's patch was almost as frightening as the thought of becoming a human vase or of being haunted by Miriam. He drew in his shoulders, sensing her presence nearby again. It was odd. He thought he'd detected her the first time Kyle had called him 'Rafe', as though he'd attracted her to him somehow and now she was circling, waiting, watching.

But why? Why would she want to haunt *him*?

'We're working on escape plans all the time,' said Tom.

Ralph snapped to attention, eager to hear them. But before any minione could speak of breaking out, the light in the room was partially eclipsed and every tiny face turned quickly to the windows.

A giant hand was closing in fast.

The Final Straw

'What's happening?' Penny cried, leaping up. Around the room, the miniones were running for the corners or grabbing hold of anything stable they could find.

Heart thumping, Ralph stood back a pace as a grubby-looking fingernail yanked the balcony windows open and some sort of tube crashed into the room. It was a long, double-width, waxed paper drinking straw. It slid in like a tank gun, knocking Rodney Coiffure off his feet. Wally ran over and dragged him to safety. For one horrible, heart-stopping second, Ralph imagined that Jack was about to indulge in a brutal game of blow football. His pulse came down a few beats when Tom said: 'Stay calm, Penny. This is how Jack communicates with us. Hang on tight to something. If he shouts, it can turn a bit blustery.'

With that, Tom, Neville and Spud O'Hare hurried over to the end of the straw, positioning themselves just behind the opening.

With a whoosh like an express train going past, Jack's voice came rumbling out. 'Wakey! Wakey!'

Ralph's hair seemed to double in length as the power

of the blast tried to tug it from its roots. The corned beef wind that was Jack Bilt's breath picked him up as though he were a weightless leaf, and sent him tumbling across the floor. He grabbed for the corner of a mattress but missed, hitting the far wall with a painful thud. When he opened his eyes, he saw Tom standing at the mouth of the straw, bellowing up it through his cupped hands. 'What do you want, Jack?' He dived aside as Jack replied, *'Smells.'*

Tom came back, this time accompanied by Spud and Neville. To Ralph's astonishment, Neville gave Spud a quick leg up and pushed the roofer into the straw. Spud punched a chisel through the paper wall, put his head down and held on tight.

'Smells? We don't understand,' hailed Tom.

'Stinkies,' said Jack, making Spud O'Hare flip like a sock on a washing line. Somehow, the roofer managed to hang on and even had time to crawl further up the straw and hammer in another chisel hold. 'I want odours. Stenches. Reeks galore. It's pegs on noses for you little worms. This is a job for *Mummy*. Got it?'

'You mean Penny?' Tom replied, stalling for time.

'I mean Mrs Pretty Penny Perfect,' Jack bellowed. The chandelier, already swinging on its chains, looped so high that it crashed loudly against the ceiling, blazing a shower of glass to the floor.

Still Spud O'Hare climbed up the straw. He was over the threshold of the balcony now.

'Knocker's nobbled,' Jack railed. 'Drugged. Dogged out. Sherried like a bloomin' trifle, he is. She meant to do me in, didn't she? Oh yes. You tell Mrs Bake-Me-a-Cake to make the house reek like a wrestler's armpit or her boy goes into the Unlucky Dip.'

Ralph heard a glassy clink.

'That's Jack, tapping the tank,' said Tom. 'Ralph, he needs you to come to the balcony.'

Ralph hobbled across. His ribs were on fire and his ankle was throbbing. Neville helped him on, telling him to look at Jack, not the straw. Spud was nearly halfway up it, between the outer wall of Miniville and the side of the aquarium.

To Ralph's horror, Jack slammed a sweet jar on the trestle table. The one full of nail clippings, from the cellar. He unscrewed the lid and waved a lollipop stick. Stuck to its end was a small chunk of corned beef. 'See this?' he boomed. 'This is what happens if Mummy doesn't work.' And he plunged the lolly stick into the clippings, stabbing and stirring and finally pulling out. Ralph turned away with his hands to his face. All that was left of the meat were strands.

'All right, Jack, she'll do it,' Tom shouted.

'I'll be sniffing,' said the builder, pressing his hideous nostrils to the tank. 'Don't get lazy, Jenks.'

'The work's almost done. The house is ready. You can't keep us here for ever, Jack.'

'I'll keep you as long as I like,' Jack roared. 'You snivelling little—'

Suddenly, he paused and narrowed his eyes. Ralph filled up with terror. For he knew that Jack had spotted something, and that something could only be the tiny shadow of an Irish roofer climbing up a straw made suddenly transparent by a narrow chink of sunlight from the garden outside.

'No,' Ralph cried, as he saw Jack pick up the magnifying glass and hold it across the path of the light, focusing the rays to a laser-fine point. Within seconds, the straw was smoking and buckling. The tiny shadow inside it wriggled.

'Jack, no!' Tom shouted.

At its centre, the straw burst into flame. It wilted and quickly dissolved into two. The minute figure of Spud O'Hare fell what, for him, must have been the best part of twenty feet. All Ralph could think of as he watched Spud drop, was spiders. How many had he caught on paper tissues and floated out of the bathroom window, reasoning that something as light as a spider wouldn't hit the ground so very hard?

Spud O'Hare, when he hit, was lucky to survive. In his youth, Ralph would discover later, Spud had served in the Royal Marines and knew how to land a parachute safely. Clutching to a canopy of burning straw, he glided, rather than fell, to earth. He landed heavily on the soles of his feet, collapsed and rolled sideways, into the base of the dying tree. The damp weeds growing up around the walls of Miniville snuffed out the flames that were licking at his jacket and combat trousers. He was knocked out, and that was his escape attempt done.

Ralph sank to the balcony floor, holding himself in a very tight ball. The dangers involved in the attempted break out had brought the scale of their predicament sharply into focus. A growing tide of nausea reached his throat and a bubble of vomit burnt against his palate. Kyle was right, Jack was a madman. He could keep them here till the day they died. They were helpless mice in a cage called Miniville.

There was no escape.

A Ghostly Encounter

'Tom, why can't we just break the glass? Throw a brick at it. Smash our way out?'

Penny was sitting on the edge of her mattress, knees drawn up, looking through the window at the dark wall of the tank. Several hours had passed since Spud O'Hare's fall. The roofer, once revived, had managed to stagger back inside the house, where he was quickly attended to by Mrs Spink. She had once been a country midwife and knew a thing or two about basic first aid. She diagnosed a broken collarbone and put Spud's arm into a makeshift sling she had cut from Neville's carpentry apron. Spud had not returned to his leaky roof that day. But the strange practice of Miniville deterioration work had carried on in double shifts throughout the afternoon until Jack had ended the punishing schedule by throwing the blue sheet over the tank, just as though he'd covered up his parrot for the night. Barring Penny, Ralph and the gutsy Tom Jenks, all the other miniones, including Spud, had fallen into an exhausted sleep.

'The tank walls are thicker than you think,' Tom

explained, eventually coming round to Penny's question. He put a smoky candle on the boards beside her. Its flame sent long shadows snaking up the walls and arcing across the plaster-cracked ceiling. 'We've tried hammers, iron spikes, battering rams, fire. Nothing comes close to cracking it.'

'What about drills?' Ralph said quickly. He was propped up on one elbow next to his mum. He'd seen Neville use a power drill that very afternoon to weaken and crack a floorboard joist. Someone must have tried a *drill*. Surely.

Tom unbuttoned the neck of his boiler suit. He looked tired and overworked. Stressed, Ralph thought; disappointed that Spud had not succeeded. Nodding, he said, 'We used a diamond-tipped bit at the highest speed possible. It was like trying to dig a tunnel through an iceberg with a toothpick; it barely scratched the surface. We'd need explosives to really break through.' He adjusted his position to untie his boots. 'We were hoping we might get lucky with the sealant—'

'Sealant?' Penny queried, holding her nose as a waft of cold air brought a foul-smelling current into her nostrils. The house in general smelt pretty awful. Having been threatened with a nose like 'Pinocchio' if she didn't start making 'eggy odours', Penny had asked if the toilet door might be left open for a while until she could think of ways to make a safer stink. Tom's sweating feet were, strangely, not the answer.

Throwing his laces wide he said, 'Those beads of silicone you see around baths. It's used in fish tanks to seal the joins and make them watertight. We stripped some back from a likely-looking corner, but we couldn't find a gap that was large enough to slip through.'

Ralph sighed and flopped back against his pillow (a tasselled cushion that smelt like the middle of an old dog's blanket). Normally he loved a good, challenging conundrum, but he liked the safety net of answers, too. There was no back page to flip to here. This was real life and this was serious: how could the toys defeat their master? 'What about upwards? Can't we climb over?'

Tom eased off his boots and gripped them in his fingers. There were holes in three of the toes of his socks. 'Even standing on the chimney pots, the tank's too high for ladders or ropes. The first week I was here, Nev and I had a crack at making suckers for our hands and feet so we could try to scale the glass.'

'Like Spiderman?' Ralph gasped. He was born under the sign of Cancer the Crab and his eyes were living up to the tag. 'Wow. What happened?'

Tom pushed back his sleeve. His arm was a mass of

purple-yellow blotches. 'This happened. And that was with four mattresses breaking my fall. Try to get some sleep. I'll see you in the morning. If you need me, I'm the scouring pad nearest the door.'

'Goodnight,' Penny whispered, slipping almost fully-clothed under her bedsheet, the way she'd been advised to do by Mrs Spink.

Tom smiled and let his gaze linger over her face. 'I'll get you out of here. That's a promise.' He winked at Ralph. 'We'll find a way, won't we?'

'Yes,' Ralph gulped.

But he'd no idea how.

That night was the loneliest Ralph had ever known. Even though he lay snuggled up close to his mother (for the first time since he was five years old, when a thunderstorm had chased him into her bed), he couldn't break away from the utter despair of being held prisoner in a house he could fit into his bedside cupboard.

So he might have been excused for lying awake in a drowsy state of terror or a woozy state of woe, but it was neither of these moods which kept him from tipping into some relief of sleep. In the early hours of that first bleak morning, with a weak ridge of moonlight slipping through a tear in the blue plastic sheeting and knifing across the bare wooden boards, he became aware of a woman's voice.

'Rafe... Oh, Rafe... Where are you, my love?'

It floated through the house like a gathering mist.

The candle light flickered.

Ralph opened his eyes very wide indeed.

'Speak to me. Don't be a stranger, I beg you. All these years. I've been waiting so long.'

A window rattled. Ralph's shoulders froze. He made a moustache of the hem of his bedsheet and held it tightly up to his nose.

'Oh, Rafe, I just know you're here,' cried the voice.

And then came the sound of dainty sobbing.

'Jemima?' Ralph whispered. 'Is that you?'

What remained of the chandelier clinked.

A door creaked.

The candle light went out.

'Miriam?' Ralph squeaked, barely moving his lips. But that tiniest of verbal acknowledgement seemed to be all the contact required to call the Miniville ghost into being. Within seconds, a current of air had dropped through the ceiling and was thickening into a swirling cloud. The cloud funnelled to a point just below the chandelier, then began to descend to the floor in a column. Although Ralph had not long visited the toilet, his body was screaming that he really ought to think about going again. Now.

'Mum,' he tried to say, but the word seemed as frightened to rise up as he was.

And so there he lay, tongue-tied, *glued*…while a spectre materialised at the foot of his bed.

A Ray of Hope

As hauntings went – those which Ralph had read about at any rate – it wasn't quite the expected thing.

'My darling,' the ghost said brightly and opened her shimmering arms to him.

Ralph's bedsheet immediately flapped aside. For shame! How glad was he that everyone in Miniville slept with their clothes on. Drawing his knees up tight to his chest, he tried again to call to his mother. But Penny was asleep and Ralph couldn't jolt her. He felt the way he did when a nightmare gripped him: in another dimension, unable to move.

Yet, apparently, he could. With no conspicuous effort – no ropes, no tackle, no mirrors of any kind – his body was swept upright, onto his feet.

'Rafe…' the apparition implored, floating like a giant sea anemone before him.

Ralph covered his face. He didn't like this. Why had the ghost picked on *him* to haunt? And why did she insist on calling him 'Rafe', just like Kyle Salter did? Just his luck if she turned out to be Kyle's great-great-long-dead aunt or something.

'Wh-wh-what do you want?' he spluttered, risking a peek through the cracks of his fingers.

The ghost blinked, cocked her nose and turned away sniffily – 'petulantly' Ralph's mum would have said. He'd learnt this word during a crushing defeat at *Scrabble* when his mum had not only cleared her tiles but scored huge triple points by adding 'ulantly' to his trifling, five-point-scoring, 'pet'. Right now, things were well beyond *Scrabble*. Ralph's bloodstream was in top gear and racing. And somewhat worryingly, despite her huffy mannerisms, he had the strange sensation that Miriam *liked* him. This was so weird. Ralph had never had a girlfriend and didn't really want one. But he'd never expected his first taste of romance to begin with a pretty, flirtatious phantom.

And she *was* pretty. Extremely pretty, if a little ashen (but then, she *was* dead). Her small, round face was set alight by her sparkling doe eyes. The bob of her hair and the straight-cut fringe gave her an innocent, boyish appearance, but she was clearly a stylish, elegant young woman, probably no more than seventeen years old and slimmer than a blade of fresh spring grass. She wore a long white dress that displayed no curves (not that Ralph really knew about curves) which seemed to be practically bandaged to her body. It stopped below her knee in a sea of fringes that whispered when she turned or cocked her hip.

Swush. She cocked her hip now. 'I suppose it's too much to ask, why you chose a giddy thing like Cecily above me?'

'Pardon?' said Ralph. Who the heck was Cecily?

'Oh,' went Miriam, pressing the back of one hand to her forehead. 'Even now you have to tease and taunt me. Why were you always such a cad to me, Rafe?'

Ralph opened his mouth and shut it again. He'd done this twice, before a sentence tumbled out. 'I'm s-sorry,' he said as politely as he could, 'but I think you've mixed me up with someone else. This isn't my house. I don't really live here. And I don't know anyone called Cecily, either.'

Miriam made a gesture of disbelief and turned away with her back to him now. When she tilted her head to look back across her shoulder, she was puffing away at the longest cigarette holder Ralph had ever seen. 'How could you leave me on our wedding day, you bounder?' She blew a smoke ring that passed right through his face.

'I didn't,' said Ralph. 'I'm only twelve.'

'Hah!' exclaimed Miriam, laying a gloved hand flat across her breast. 'My poor heart, broken like a piece of crystal. Why should I forgive you, you faithless rake? If only you weren't so devilishly handsome.'

'Help!' Ralph shrieked as she turned to face him, batting her ghostly eyelids so fast that it felt as if butterflies were fanning his face. Through her wispy body, he could see the far wall in perfect detail. Goosebumps rose on his trembling forearms. And if his hair had not been spiky in the first place, it was certainly doing a really good hedgehog show now.

Miriam raised a hand to his face. She made a stroking movement but didn't quite touch. Ralph felt as though a shower of ice cold glitter or a small comet had just flown by. 'You do seem a little youthful,' she said, 'without your moustache and monocle. But then you always were a frivolous thing. Oh Rafe, tell me you've come back for ever. Stop teasing. Show me your manly form.'

Ralph made a noise like a squealing rat.

'Say you love me. Show me the ring.'

'What ring? I haven't got a ring,' Ralph tweeted. In panic, he fumbled around in his pockets. Perhaps if he showed her there was nothing there but a pebble and a conker and an old laggy band and... 'All I've got is this.'

He opened his hand. And lo and behold and wouldn't you know it, there in his palm was the stone he'd taken from Jack Bilt's fridge. It twinkled in the darkness and changed colour twice, gradually shaping a soft blue halo right around Miriam's vaporous form.

The phantom gasped with delight. 'My sweetheart, it's so beautiful.' And in her joy, she threw her arms around him.

Contact. The moment Ralph had been dreading. He closed his eyes and grimaced for England, wondering if his body had now been possessed and he would turn into a woman at periodic intervals, and a priest would have to be miniaturised in to exorcise the spirit that was wrestling for his soul. But nothing quite that dramatic happened. The stone sent out a pulse of light and Miriam was propelled like a burst balloon into the cobwebs in the corner of the room.

'Oh, Rafe. You cad. How could you?' she wailed, her voice thinning out to a faraway dot as she disappeared back to humanknowswhere.

Freed from her aura, Ralph found he was able to shout without restraint. Mini-people stirred on their mini mattresses. Tom came hurrying up, pulling on a T-shirt. 'Ralph, are you OK? Are you having a nightmare?'

Ralph shook his head. 'Miriam was here.'

A look of concern passed over Tom's face.

But Ralph was no longer afraid. In fact, a sudden ray

of hope had fired his heart. He looked at the stone, bouncing its blue light off the four walls. It had power, this stone, the power to ward off ghosts. So what had it been doing in Jack Bilt's fridge?

And was it the key to defeating him?

Problems, Problems

Early next morning, Tom called a meeting of the whole house. 'Last night,' he announced, 'Ralph had a visitation – from Miriam.'

'So what's new?' Kyle grunted, faking a yawn.

'He saw her,' said Neville, knocking ash from his pipe. (Ralph wished he'd knock it against Salter's head.)

'Saw her?' Jemima gasped. Her long, fair curls shook like wallflowers in a spring breeze.

'Oh, how lovely, what's she like?' asked Mrs Spink.

'Huffy,' said Ralph. He thrust his hands into his pockets.

Mrs Spink steepled hers in a thoughtful pose. 'In the spirit world, they'd say "troubled", Ralph.'

'You're telling me,' muttered Wally, who'd been hit by a flying can just the day before and had a spreading purple bruise on his elbow to prove it.

Tom called the group to order. 'She appears to be a young society girl, aged about seventeen. We're not sure why she materialised. It seems she made a connection with Ralph and confused him with someone called 'Rafe', who we're guessing was her intended partner.'

Kyle Salter exploded with laughter.

'Be quiet. It's not funny,' Penny snapped at him.

And just for a second, the bully flinched. Ralph wondered idly if a good strong word from a loving parent early in his life might have made Kyle a different boy. He was certainly getting savaged for his bad behaviour now. Sweeping her hair firmly out of her eyes, Penny lectured him sharply. 'Ghosts don't haunt a place without good reason. There's usually some kind of tragedy involved. This Miriam girl would have died here, most likely. And from what Ralph's told me it sounds as though she was jilted by her fiancé. It's my guess she died of a broken heart.'

'Oh dear. How dreadful,' Mrs Spink said.

'Quite,' said Penny. 'If she's throwing things about, she's emotionally disturbed and might be seeking revenge on my son.'

'I don't think she was, Mum,' Ralph said quietly.

'Ralph,' his mum hissed in that not so very quiet 'please don't contradict me in company' voice.

Ralph shuffled his feet. 'It's just...I don't know. I thought she sort of liked me.'

Tom coughed into his fist. 'Your mum has a point, though, Ralph. We should be on our guard. You did zap Miriam, remember. If she wakes up somewhere with a big ghostly headache she might really start to move the furniture about.'

As if by magic, bangs and crashes of all description began to filter down from the tower room. This wasn't the first commotion Ralph had heard up there. It seemed to be Miriam's focal point, as though she was having an ongoing 'domestic' with the occupant of that strange, locked place. As the crashes settled, the wailing voice shouted, 'Belt the keeper!' or something like it. Ralph scratched his head. What *was* that deranged voice saying?

'Zapped her?'

He turned to see Kyle staring hard at him.

Salter switched his gaze to Tom, who by now had seated the stone on his palm, showing it round like a jewel on a cushion. 'Ralph took this from Jack's fridge, just before he was miniaturised. We're not sure what it is, but it repelled Miriam when she touched it. Doesn't seem to have the same effect on humans.'

Mrs Spink closed her eyes and cupped a hand above the stone, catching its radiance in her palm. It was pulsing away like an amber-coloured heart. Twice now Ralph had seen it change colour. *Was the heat making it unstable?* he wondered.

'It is a crystal. It has great energy,' said Sylvia. 'I do

not believe it is of this world.'

The electrician, Wally, leant forward to inspect it. 'Look how the light's bouncing round inside it. I think it's sparking, creating a charge.'

'It is in tune with the cosmos,' Mrs Spink pronounced.

'Dunno about that,' said Wally. 'If you ask me, it's some sort of power cell or battery. Maybe it's connected with the workings of the transgenerator.'

'Oh, well, that's *really* dandy,' said Kyle.

'Meaning?' Tom asked.

Kyle threw up a hand. 'How often do you go to your fridge?'

Neville blew a funnel of smoke from his nose. 'I take the lad's point, Tom. How long's it going to be before Jack checks t'fridge and finds out this stone thing's missing?'

'And when he does,' applauded Kyle, 'where's the first place he'll look for his 'cosmic battery'? Right here, in Miniville. Well done, Rafe, old bean, nice double whammy – bagged off the ghost and set us all up for a rumble with Jack. The only consolation is, with any luck, you'll be first in the fingernail jar.'

'But the stone was shut away in a box,' said Ralph, clocking fretful glances from the miniones around him;

Jemima's face was a mess of despair. 'He probably doesn't open it all that often.'

Which was a perfectly reasonable conclusion to arrive at, because nothing nasty had happened…yet. Kyle's logic, though, was harsh but correct. If Jack discovered the stone was missing, his list of suspects for the robbery would be short. Very short. One name, most likely. 'The boy,' R. Perfect.

Tom took a more optimistic view. 'All the same, this could still be a breakthrough. If this does turn out to be something Jack needs, we might be able to use it to our advantage.'

'How?' asked Wally. 'We're workmen, not scientists.'

Tom looked at them all in turn. 'It's possible we could do a deal with him: exchange the stone for the release of Penny, Sylvia and the children.'

'No,' said Penny, standing up, facing him. 'One out, all out. Or I don't go.'

Tom looked at her sadly.

'No,' she repeated. 'I won't go. That's final.'

Without you, thought Ralph, filling in the gaps. She won't go without you, that's what she means.

'Me, neither. I'm no kid,' growled Kyle, beating his gorilla fist against his chest. But Ralph didn't buy this act of bravado. Why, he couldn't say. Perhaps it was the greedy squint in Kyle's cold eyes when his gaze fell upon the mysterious stone? Or maybe it was just Kyle Salter, period?

Daylight flooded in.

'Time's up; he's lifted the sheet,' said Tom.

Ralph glanced through the window and saw Jack throwing the covering aside. The builder's thin, scarred face loomed close. His bloodshot eyeball searched out his workforce.

'RISE AND SHINE!' He sneezed violently and knocked the trestle table. The house shook as though a minor earthquake had hit. Spud O'Hare, with only one arm for balance, lost his footing and fell against the wall, crying out in pain as his shoulder took the impact. Penny and Mrs Spink went to him, settling him onto a nearby mattress. A slate came crashing off the roof and the vase that Luke Baker was cruelly mixed up in wobbled and toppled off the mantelpiece.

Kyle Salter dived forward and caught it.

Even Ralph, for all he hated the Salter gang, breathed a sigh of relief.

'To work,' said Tom, picking up his toolbox. 'We'll discuss this again, later. Any bright ideas about the stone, I'd like to hear them. Ralph, come on, you stick with me today. Long time since I trained an apprentice.'

And they went downstairs, into the parlour.

On the way, Tom returned the stone to Ralph and told him to keep it well out of sight. Ralph buried it deep in his hanky, in his pocket. He thought back to Tom's words about doing a deal and a terrible sadness gripped his heart. He said, 'Jack's never going to let us out of here, is he?'

Tom paused a second, then walked on. 'We need to fix a valve on this,' he said, dropping his tools beside an old-fashioned radiator.

'He can't let us out. We'll tell,' Ralph continued. 'He'll keep us here, won't he? Looking after the house? Putting doors right when they fall off their hinges. Making sure the wallpaper peels when it's supposed to. We'll be his workmen for ever, won't we? We'll *all* be Miniville ghosts.'

Tom thought about this quietly and then he said, 'During the Second World War, three captured British soldiers found a way out of their prison camp by digging a tunnel in the yard outside their hut. They covered the hole with a gymnasium horse the Germans had allowed them to exercise with. The prisoners dug for months, concealing the soil they'd scraped from the tunnel in bags suspended inside their trousers, which they shook out when they walked around the yard. All three escaped, because they were clever and had courage and because they never once stopped believing they could do it – and neither will we. Jack will slip up one day, Ralph. We'll find his weakness; this stone may be it. Keep looking. Keep believing. That's all I ask. Now, radiator.'

Ralph nodded and studied the valve. 'Is it leaking?'

'No, but it's going to. This is Miniville, remember.' Tom opened his tools and took out a wrench. He was spinning its silver-coloured jaws to size when Ralph heard a splattering noise outside.

'What's up?' asked Tom, aware that he'd lost his mate's concentration.

'Nothing. I think it's just started to rain.'

A few pudgy drops flew past the window.

'Rain?' said Tom.

Ralph looked again. Yes, a heavy shower was definitely coming down.

And then the dumb gong banged inside his head…

…erm, Ralph, how can it rain inside a fish tank?

Water! Water!

'WATER!' Tom yelled at the top of his voice, clanking the side of his toolbox with the wrench. To Ralph's amazement, he quickly turned the box over and spilt the contents with a loud, metallic clatter.

Neville and Kyle burst into the room – Neville with a big white plastic bag, Kyle with the saved Luke Baker vase. Tom gave a disapproving frown but all Kyle said was, 'He's my mate, it's what he would have wanted.' He yanked the front door open, pounded down the steps and into the rain, Neville close behind.

'What's going on?' asked Ralph.

'Grab anything you can find that holds water,' said Tom. 'Hurry, Ralph, he doesn't give us long.' And *he* dashed into the downpour, too.

By now a whole string of water-gatherers had begun to scurry past with pails and buckets and tin cans and jars. Mrs Spink came through in her stockinged feet, carrying her Wellington boots at arms length.

Ralph stopped her by the door. 'Mrs Spink, what's happening?'

She pointed outside. The 'rain' was belting down,

sluicing through a hole in the down pipe by the door, splattering the mane of a lion statue. 'This is how we gather fresh water, dear. Jack sprays us now and then from his watering can.'

His *watering* can? Ralph took a step back. 'But he spits in it. And Knocker slobbers his tongue round the rose. And you can't drink water that's been in your *boots*.'

'It's better than going thirsty, dear.' And away she went, with her wellies at the ready.

Ralph couldn't believe it. He glanced into the thin strip of Miniville garden and saw the miniones splashing about, drenched to the skin, holding high their pots and vessels, trying to guess where Jack would tilt the can next. It was shameful and humiliating. Watered on, like weeds. And dangerous, too. For if Jack decided to tilt the can sharply, the water droplets exploded like bombs off the bottom of the tank. Neville was knocked off his feet by such a blast and swilled into a pool of free-standing water. He was rescued by the one-eyed decorator, Sam. Ralph didn't fancy it one little bit, but for the good of the group he knew he'd have to join in and get soaked too. There was just one problem. 'I don't have anything to collect water in,' he shouted.

But as he turned to search, a container appeared. It was a rounded glass lampshade in the shape of a large white raspberry, like the type he'd seen in his grandma's bathroom. And it was floating.

Just floating.

In mid-air.

Out of nowhere came a woman's voice. 'So, Rafe, we're alone again.'

Ralph's feet fused to the floor. 'M-miriam, I th-thought you'd gone away?' he stammered, making slow circular movements of his eyes. This time, the ghost hadn't shown herself. But her prickly presence was all too apparent. And Ralph didn't like the way she was bouncing that shade. It reminded him of a demon bowler preparing to unleash a wicket-breaking delivery, the 'wicket' in this case being his head.

'I see. Is that what you want?' she huffed, raising the hairs on the back of his neck like a row of magnetised iron filings.

Ralph shut his eyes and ground his teeth. He didn't want to be haunted, but he did have some sympathy for Miriam's cause. It *was* her house they'd invaded, after all. He tried to give a tactful answer. 'I didn't mean to send you flying. I didn't know it would happen. It was just a sort of accident, sorry.'

'Hmph,' she went.

Ralph's ear tips froze. 'I mean it,' he squeaked.

'Please believe me. We just...I just...want you to be happy.'

Aw, that sounded totally naff, but Miriam did not react aggressively. In fact, she seemed rather pleased by the remark. 'Oh Rafe,' she said with a rush of cold air that made the strands of his fringe beat fast, like cilia. 'Stay with me forever. That would make me happy.'

The lampshade bobbled. The tools on the floor began to dance. Ralph made a cry like a startled blackbird. He didn't like this. He'd always hated that film *Mary Poppins* – and here he was, starring in a real-life version.

'I can't,' he said. 'I don't belong here, Miriam. I'm—'

'Ralph, come on,' Tom called from outside.

'Oh!' went Miriam, annoyed by the intrusion. A rubber-handled hammer rose up off the floor.

'Don't!' Ralph cried as the hammer went spinning towards Tom's head. Luckily, it clipped the inner frame of the door and dropped to the floor with no damage done.

'Who are all these people in our house?' the ghost tutted.

Ralph clenched his fists and blew a little steam. He'd had enough of this. This ghost needed...busting. 'Miriam, I command you...come forth!'

That sounded even naffer than the previous line – yet surprisingly, it worked. There was a pause, then the beautiful ghost shimmered forth. Despite her general washed-out appearance, she seemed to be a deeper shade of grey around the cheeks.

'It's not *our* house. It's *your* house,' Ralph told her. 'We don't want to be here. We're trying to escape. We're being held prisoner by a man called Jack. You must have seen him?'

'The ogre?' she queried, looking for the first time vulnerable – and frightened.

'Yes. No. Sort of. Yes. He's normal size, really; he just made you tiny. He's stolen you from Yorkshire. *He's* the one you should throw things at. He's going to put you on display at the seaside, Miriam.'

'Oh, how I love the sea air,' she breezed. 'Do you remember when we walked along the promenade at Eastbourne?'

Ralph slapped a hand across his eyes. 'Miriam, I'm not *your* Rafe.'

There was a pause. Miriam turned away, stage left. 'Oh, I know,' she said crossly, tossing him the lampshade. Ralph fumbled the catch but managed to keep a grip. He glanced outside. He could still gather water, if he was quick.

'I have to haunt *someone*. It's my job,' Miriam sighed. 'It's far more interesting if I pretend you're him.' She toyed with a string of pearls around her neck, letting them spill through her fingers as she spoke. 'I suppose you're going to leave me, now, just like he did?'

'I can't. I told you, we're trapped in here.'

Miriam twizzled a bone china hand and practised some wraith-like ballet steps. 'Then we are equals, for I am trapped also.'

'But you're a ghost,' Ralph said as she pirouetted round him. 'You can go where you like. You can walk through walls if you—'

Bingo. Suddenly, an idea struck him. An idea so bizarre and yet so very neat that he wondered how his brain could have missed it before. Could the ghost be the opening they were looking for? 'Miriam, can I ask you a question?'

'You'd like to dance a Charleston?'

'No,' Ralph said.

'You want to ask for my hand in marriage?'

'No,' Ralph said. 'It's about being a ghost.'

'I'm so lonely,' she sniffed, laying a hand across her breast.

'You don't have to be,' said Ralph, making her pout. 'Your Rafe is out there somewhere, isn't he?'

Miriam flicked her eyes to one side.

Ralph pointed to the outside world. 'All you have to do is go and look for him, don't you? Erm, can you walk through glass?'

So Close...

'Of course,' Miriam said, waving her arms with a theatrical flourish. 'I can pass through any kind of medium, Rafe. I can fly as well.' And with a whoosh that swept the dust into a vortex, she took off and circled the chandelier.

Meanwhile, from the garden, Tom was shouting: 'Ralph? What are you doing? Come on. We need you.'

Ralph raised one hand, gesturing for patience. If he could just keep Miriam on the floor for a moment, all their problems might be solved. As she came back to hover in front of him he said, 'Miriam, listen to me. I think I can help you.'

'With my deportment?' she said, whisking the lampshade off him again and prancing back and forth with it balanced on her head.

'No. I can help you escape back to Yorkshire, away from us, away from the ogre. All you have to do is walk through the glass and steal his watch.'

Miriam flexed her knees and put out her arms like the wings of an aeroplane. 'Go outside?' she queried.

'Yes,' Ralph said.

'I can't, my love.'

'But you just said you could. You said you could pass through glass.'

'Oh, Rafey, don't be such a bore. You know perfectly well why I can't go out. I'm doomed to haunt this house. My spirit is tied to these horrible walls. If I pass beyond them, I'll surely die.'

'But you're already dead!'

'Not dead dead,' she tutted.

'How dead do you have to be before you snuff it?'

Miriam's eyelids fluttered like moths. 'If I walk beyond these walls, terrible forces will be unleashed. You wouldn't want to see me in danger would you, Rafe?'

'I suppose not,' he said, his spirits sinking. For a moment, there, things had seemed so promising. But Miriam was right. Why should her 'life' be put at risk, just because she wasn't of this world?

'Besides,' she said gaily, tickling his chin with the glitter-cold again, 'I have to await my Rafe's return.'

But he'll never come back, Ralph thought sadly. *That was how it was with ghosts, wasn't it? The people they were waiting for never came back.* Which begged the question... 'Who's upstairs in the tower room, then? We thought *that* was your Rafe, lighting candles for you.'

'Him?' Miriam gave a snort of displeasure. 'That old fool? I shall curdle his blood if he doesn't leave soon.'

'You mean he's real?'

'You mean I'm not?'

Ralph decided not to pursue this. Interesting as the concept was, he wasn't quite ready for a philosophical argument with a neurotic ghost. 'Who is he?'

'Oh, Rafey. How should I know? He just appeared. Like you. Like the others.'

He's a *minione*? thought Ralph. 'What does he look like?'

'Old,' she said unhelpfully. 'A horrible gargoyle. He never stops scribbling on my walls. And oh, those dreadful squeaky chains. This way, that way, he drags them every way. I can't get a wink of sleep in there. Every night I have to come here and float in the parlour.'

'Why is Jack keeping him locked away?'

'Because he's annoying.'

'Miriam?'

'He is. He never stops shouting, Rafe.'

'What does he say? Do you know? I can't tell. It sounds like 'Belt a teacher,' but what is it really?'

Miriam flapped a hand. 'Oh, I don't know.'

'Please, Miriam. It might be important.'

'It's nonsense, Rafey. Gobbledygook.'

'It doesn't matter. Please, just tell me.'

'Oh, very well. He says—'

Annoyingly, before Miriam could answer, Rodney Coiffure burst into the parlour asking had the water collection finished?

With a *pop!* Miriam disappeared back into her ghost-world. Unsupported, the lampshade dropped. Just in time, Ralph put out his hands and caught it.

'Ingenious choice,' said Rodney. He showed Ralph the baseball cap he intended using as his water bowl. Then he dashed into the 'rain' with Ralph close behind him.

The rose was sprinkling out the last of its contents. By now, the miniones were walking dishcloths. Ralph couldn't understand why Tom hadn't told them to forget catching water and just fill their containers from the free-standing pool they were wading around in. That question was answered when Jack produced a grimy-looking bathroom sponge and drove it round the base of the tank to soak up any excess puddles. The miniones dived into the house for cover. But Ralph, inexperienced in Miniville procedure, was picked up on a tidal wave and swept against the front wall of the aquarium. He bounced off the glass and his lampshade broke into four clean pieces. It was barely a tenth full.

Jack hurled the plastic watering can aside. 'GIT BACK TO WORK, YOU LOAFERS,' he boomed and blew a thick cloud of cigarette smoke over them. It choked and burned in the back of Ralph's throat. Coughing uncontrollably, he fell to his knees. Haunted, soaked and now poisoned by tar, he couldn't even cry 'I hate you' any more.

And yet, bright moments lay on the horizon. For, as the cloud of smoke began to disperse and Jack disappeared towards Annie's kitchen, Ralph found himself at the face of the tank, about to watch a comedy caper unfold, a bizarre little episode that would have all manner of outcomes and effects – ultimately leading to his passage out of Miniville…

Anyone for toast?

It went like this: Jack had grilled some toast for breakfast. The warm, crisp smell of it hung in the air, stirring the hunger bunnies in Ralph's stomach (he'd eaten very little since he'd been shrivelled and couldn't face the prospect of sugar beads for breakfast). The toast was on a plate on the arm of the sofa. Ralph had zero chance of reaching it, of course, but the same could not be said of Knocker. With a lurch more in common with a hog than a dog, he leapt onto the couch, tipping the plate and its contents off. Down he jumped again, and in doing so, somehow managed to spear half a slice of toast with his wooden leg. He twizzled it impatiently, left and right. It was a pitiful sight and Ralph couldn't help laughing. He had seen dogs chasing their tails before, but never their master's freshly-grilled breakfast. Round and round and round went Knocker, flicking out his stick as he picked up speed. He was on his tenth spin and seriously twizzle-dizzy when the toast worked its way to the end of the stick and...

Wheee... it winged towards Ralph like a giant brown frisbee...

Instinctively, he covered his face, forgetting there was a thick glass barrier protecting him.

Splat. Knocker and the room were obscured from view as the toast gummed itself, marmalade-side first, to the wall of the tank.

Ralph ran sideways to get a clearer view and was just in time to see Jack march in, tread on the edge of the plate, and send it and the second slice of toast spinning. *Splop.* It landed on the builder's hat.

Jack's words were like a nuclear explosion, far too loud to be understood, but the kick he aimed at Knocker's head needed no explaining. The terrier veered away just in time and scuttled underneath the trestle table. In two strides, Jack was by the tank.

Ralph backed away, fear coursing through his heart. He'd been spotted, he knew, but he was too proud to run.

'You,' the giant builder rumbled. Through the parting curtains of his worm-thin lips his teeth showed up like a row of cracked tiles. He looked at the toast and his gaze grew darker. Then, in one terrifying lunge, he slapped his bony hand flat against the bread and sponged it along the wall of the tank.

Ralph was terrified. He had once had a dream where he was trapped in a car while a clown washed the windscreen with orange-coloured acid. If a nightmare could be lived through, this came close. He dodged left. He dodged right. But whichever way he went, the marmalade followed, until it was smeared all over the glass and the toast was thinning out and turning soggy. Jack grimaced as margarine squirted down his wrist. He scooped up the slice and hurled it, palm first, into the tank.

Ralph braced himself. He had nowhere to run. No place to hide. It was Dinosaur Day and the meteor was coming. He waited for his young life to flash before him, hoping he'd remember the fluky headed goal he'd scored in the playground at primary school when Kyle Salter (of all people) had been between the posts. But, as the blanket bomb of breakfast came slapping down, nothing flashed or sparked or played out before him. He waited three seconds, then opened his eyes. Ground level was a sea of brown and orange. He was standing at its centre, in the hole that Knocker had punched with his stick.

'Drat,' Jack snorted. 'Missed.' He cracked his knuckles and lurched away.

Penny's voice shouted down from the balcony window: 'Ralph! Oh my goodness! Are you OK?'

Ralph freed his foot from a slimy blob of marmalade and waved back to show he was sticky, but safe.

Tom, Neville and Wally were all outside now, all looking on in wonder at the toast. Ralph flicked a splat of margarine out of his hair and stepped towards Tom's outstretched hand. The toast had the texture of a well-worn mattress. It was like walking on the skin of a thick rice pudding. He was on his knees twice before the swamp was crossed.

'This is champion,' said Neville, extending a tape measure around the crust. 'This'll keep us fed for a good three days.'

Ralph screwed up his face. 'You're not going to eat it?'

'Got to,' said Wally, 'or the flies will come.' He broke a crumb or two off the crust and gobbled it up like a hungry sparrow.

Ralph's stomach rolled. He looked at Tom who said to Neville, 'Let's cut it up and get it inside.'

'Aye,' said the carpenter, sizing up the job.

He took a small tenon saw from his belt.

To Ralph's surprise, the toast didn't taste too bad. It had landed dry side down, so apart from a few globs of garden mud and the sickening thought of Jack's nicotined fingers staining every grain of polished wheat, the 'grand dinner' (as Kyle Salter referred to it) was reasonably enjoyable. It was a strange sight to witness, twelve people (Miriam didn't attend) sitting around the edge of a chunk of bread, nibbling their way towards its centre.

It was during the dessert course, while the miniones were munching through the piece of toast with the heaviest concentration of unspread marmalade, that Ralph told Tom about his second clash with Miriam.

'She came again?' Tom said, keeping his voice low.

Ralph nodded, stifling a burp. 'That's why I was late collecting water. She told me about the tower room. She says it's not a ghost in there, it's a man.'

Tom stopped eating. He slowly wiped his lip. 'Did you ask her about him?'

'Yes, she said—'

'I say, Rafe, old chap, pass the salt, would you?'

Ralph instinctively looked for it, tutting when he realised he was being taunted – by Kyle Salter, who else?

Salter, who ate like a chimpanzee (and sounded like one too), passed a hand across an open mouth that was churning toast into cardboard-coloured slop. 'This a private conversation or can anyone join in?'

Why do you want to know? thought Ralph. That selfish glare was back in Kyle's eyes, the one Ralph didn't trust. He glanced at Tom, who spoke up freely: 'Ralph's learnt that the tenant upstairs is human.'

Nearly everyone stopped eating.

'Told you,' said Salter, a cluster bomb of spittle and undigested bread falling from between his twisted teeth.

'Then why's he locked up? Why's he chained?' people asked.

Ralph was about to say he didn't know, when his ear drums were battered by a piercing scream from Jemima Culvery.

She jumped up and pressed back against the wall, wagging a flaky arm towards the window.

Ralph's heart leapt. Climbing the marmaladed wall of the tank were a host of unmistakeable shapes. Black, fast-moving, six-legged.

Ants.

A Visitor Calls

There must have been ten of them, possibly fifteen, winding out like a solar flare from the biggest smear of visible grease.

In the panic-stricken mayhem that followed, the men were quickly on their feet, with Tom, as usual, giving the orders. 'Wally, fetch the spears. Kyle, light the torches.'

For once, Kyle Salter didn't argue. He hurried across the room to where a small stack of makeshift torches lay. They were made from tin cans stuck onto broom handles, with rolled-up cardboard tubes for wicks. Using the cigarette lighter he'd once tried to singe Ralph's hairline with, he lit one and threw it across to Neville.

'I'll guard t'front door,' Neville said bravely and was halfway to the landing when Ralph cried, 'Stop. You're not going to kill them, are you?'

Neville stumbled to a halt. Confused, he looked to Tom for guidance.

Tom said, 'What are you talking about, Ralph?'

'They can save us. They can take us out of here.'

'*What?*' screeched Jemima. 'Is he mental or something?'

'Ralph, please, not now,' his mum gulped. She knew about his passion for ants, of course, but their presence here terrified her as much as anyone. They were now more than halfway up the tank wall, flicking their antennae as if they suspected there were rewards far greater than marmalade inside. Penny pulled the collar of her blouse to her neck and tried to draw Ralph closer to her.

Belligerently, he broke away. 'I know about ants,' he said, glancing around the group for support. 'They work in teams. They're organised and clever. If they come into the tank, they'll leave a marked trail to guide themselves out again.'

'And you think we can hitch a lift?' asked Wally.

'They can carry twenty times their own weight,' Ralph said.

'He's mad,' wailed Jemima. 'Don't listen to him. I'm not going to ride out of here on an ant.'

'It's a daring idea,' said Rodney.

'So is flying out on a bluebottle,' said Kyle. 'I don't think ants with their acid spit and their nice sharp *mandibles* are going to be keen to be lassoed, do you?' He aimed a challenging glare at Tom.

Tom switched his spear from one hand to the other.

His indecision only made Kyle more bolshie. 'Come

on! We don't have time for this! If their army marches into this house, they'll mince us.' His torch flared brightly and he whipped away.

Wally backed him up. Weighing his spear like a javelin he said, 'He's right, Tom. We don't have time to think this through. We have no choice. We have to fight.'

'I wouldn't be too sure about that now,' said Spud. He pointed through the balcony window.

Jack had appeared at the front of the tank. He had a handkerchief tied across his nose and mouth and in his hands was an old-fashioned greenhouse puffer with a pointed nozzle and a brass pumping rod. He'd spotted the trail of ants and was zapping them with clouds of toxic, yellow vapour. One by one, the creatures were losing their grip and falling, distressed, to the trestle table. There was a wild, wild look in the builder's eyes, and Ralph remembered now how skittish he'd been when ants had been mentioned outside Annie's house. He clearly intended to take no prisoners.

The sight of those poisoned, wriggling bodies was enough to sicken anyone, even Kyle Salter. But as the rest of the miniones turned away in pity, he had to be the one to open his mouth. 'Done us a favour for once,' he said, trying to suffocate his torch against the wall of the house.

'You're pathetic,' Ralph said, a wave of anger rising inside him. 'Ants are twice as smart as you.'

Salter turned, his torch still lit. 'What's that, mummy's boy?'

And that was it. Ralph went for him. He didn't care that Kyle was twice his size and had fire in his grip and poison in his heart, he just bundled on into him and took him down, pummelling his arms across the bully's chest as though he was practising a swimming stroke.

'Ralph!' his mother cried in shock.

It took three men to peel the boys apart.

Tom held Salter gurgling by the collar. 'Let me at him. I'll tear his pointy ears off.' Lunging forward against Tom's grip, he swung a punch that missed Ralph's chin by a draught.

'Ease off, lad. Save it for Jack,' said Neville, helping Tom push Kyle away.

'You've gone soft,' Kyle spluttered. 'All of you.' He spat at Ralph and backed off, pointing.

But before anyone could scold him for that, there came a sound like the drone of an articulated truck and Knocker started barking loudly.

'What was that?' said Penny, looking up. Her ears,

many times smaller than the norm, could not determine the jangle of a giant's doorbell. But the more experienced miniones knew it.

'Door,' muttered Wally. 'Someone's at the door.'

Ralph looked at Jack. The builder had turned his head. His last shot of poison had gone hopelessly astray. One surviving, dizzy-looking ant fell to the table and staggered away.

Ralph sent it a mental prayer. Get well. Go back to the nest. Bring others.

Tom, meanwhile, was breathing a hopeful prayer of his own. 'Go on-nn, Jack, go to the door.'

The builder clicked his fingers at Knocker – then walked away, leaving the tank uncovered.

'Men, to the tank wall. Now!' Tom ordered.

'What's happening?' said Penny, cradling Jemima.

'Our landlord's got a visitor,' Tom said keenly. 'And Jack's forgotten to cover us up.' He picked up the only saucepan they possessed and smacked it hard against the house wall. 'Grab anything that makes a noise. Let's go.' And he was gone, waving the others to follow.

Across the space, Kyle Salter and Ralph faced up.

'You leave him alone,' Penny Perfect warned. 'Mummy's boy he might be, but mummies protect their young, remember?'

'I'll get you,' Salter mouthed at Ralph. And he picked up the torch he'd dropped in the fight, re-lit it properly and joined the flow of bodies.

'I don't know why they're bothering,' Jemima whittled, shivering into Penny's arms. 'Whoever it is will only end up shrunk like the rest of us.'

Hearing the thud of multiple footsteps, Ralph turned to see who the visitor could be. He gasped out loud when he recognised the face.

Detective Inspector Nicholas Bone had followed Jack in.

Seen at Last

Despite his mother's protests about toxic fallout from garden puffers, Ralph snatched up a loose piece of firewood and was at the tank wall in a matter of seconds. With an arm across his mouth to protect his lungs from the choking sulphur air, he found a space among the row of miniones and walloped the aquarium with everything he'd got.

To the giants in the room it must have sounded no louder than a fairy sneezing, for neither of them cast their eye towards the tank, and to Ralph's dismay, Bone turned his attention first to *The Frisker*, circling the thing like a member of the public invited to inspect a magician's cabinet.

Jack was straight into pantomime mode, dancing, half-bent, wringing his hands. He reminded Ralph of the creature, Gollum, from *The Lord of the Rings*, always sucking up, never to be trusted. He touched a button. The trestle table buzzed to the hum of *The Frisker's* motor, its bright lights raced each other round the frame.

Bone seemed unimpressed. Pursing his lips like a

small pair of bellows, he turned a half-circle and rumbled out a question (it was easy to guess from the tone of his voice). And now his watery, policeman's eyes did begin to pan every corner of the room.

'Louder,' Tom shouted to the cast of miniones. 'We've got to make ourselves heard.' And he banged the sheer wall of glass so hard that the body of his saucepan flew off the handle.

Ralph hammered away with all his might, till sweat beads were trickling into his eyes and his biceps were angry, complaining and sore. But it was working. Bone had raised a hand to his ear and was fiddling with something just inside the shell. Ralph realised at once it was a hearing aid. *Please*, he begged all the powers of creation, *make him turn it up really loud*. He whacked the glass with extra force.

The policeman listened attentively for a moment, then, with a puzzled frown, he turned towards the tank.

Triumph.

Surely?

He must see.

No.

Quicker than a ferret down a rabbit hole, Jack had nipped in front of the detective, blocking Bone's view of that side of the room. He minced a little more and waggled a mug. 'Tea, Inspector?'

Bone appeared to say a sharp, 'No, thank you.' He dipped a hand inside his jacket and retrieved what looked to be a piece of newsprint.

As he unfolded it, Jack stepped sideways towards the sofa and picked up the plastic covering sheet. Snarling at Knocker to 'git out of the way', he casually turned from Bone and threw the sheet loosely over the tank, plunging the miniones into darkness.

'Blast,' said Tom, his anger illumined by the flare of the torches.

'What now?' said Sam.

The plumber looked up at the plastic sky. 'There's a hole in it,' he muttered.

'Great,' said Kyle. 'Our very own ozone hole.'

'What are you thinking?' asked Wally, wiping sweat off his brow.

Tom looked at the dripping branches of the tree. 'Torch it,' he said. 'Set it alight. The wet wood will smoke and the air hole will draw the fumes up and out. Let's send our policeman a signal, shall we?' He looked at the rest of the dumbfounded miniones.

Neville tightened his fist. 'Aye, do it,' he said.

So Kyle played his torch among the dried, dead wood of the lowest branches, turning them from grey to a dancing gold. The flames swept inwards towards the trunk. The wood split and crackled and the flame trails merged. *Whumph*. With a flash and a surge of heat, the tree began to burn. A coil of smoke rose out of the flames and headed towards the hole above.

By now, Ralph had run further down the tank towards a thin sliver of natural light. If he shut one eye and squinted hard, Jack and the Inspector were still just visible through a slit in the sheet.

'What's happening?' asked Tom.

'They're just talking,' said Ralph. But in his heart he knew it was more than that. Bone's facial expression was dark and distrustful. He had thrust the piece of newsprint under Jack's nose and was clearly interrogating the builder about it. Ralph's heart began to pound. This had to be to do with Professor Collonges. But what could Bone be saying to Jack? Carefully observing their body movements, Ralph imagined it went like this:

Bone: 'Do you know this man, Mr Bilt?' He taps his finger on the last known picture of Ambrose Collonges, genius of physics, first reported missing six weeks ago.

Jack grimaces. He shakes his head.

'You sure about that?'

Jack pushes back his sleeve. On his arm, the

strange-looking wristwatch blinks.

Bone sees it, but presses on with his inquiry. 'Take a good look at the name below the picture. Ambrose Collonges. Unusual, isn't it? Difficult to say. Even harder to forget. Wouldn't you agree, Mr Bilt?'

Jack wrinkles his nose. He has the look of a man whose collar has been felt. He smirks. He's clearly had enough of these questions.

Not so Inspector Bone. 'He's gone missing, you see, and I intend to find him, which is why I'm here, with you and your contraptions...' He bounces on his toes and starts to prod and poke, examining the ramshackle bits of invention that will one day, Jack hopes, find themselves displayed on the end of a pier.

Jack says nothing. He lets Bone wander. The policeman starts towards the Miniville project, then pauses in the very centre of the room. His nose twitches. So does Knocker's. Jack Bilt wipes some snot from his. He twists the green pyramid on his wrist, tuning in to Bone's body heat. One quick press of the red counterpart and the troublesome copper will be arresting nothing much bigger than an ant.

Bone puts his fists to his hips. He sniffs and sniffs and sniffs again. Something, somewhere is burning, he's sure of it. But he can't decide what or where. He stares at the tank and presses Jack again. 'During the course of my investigations, I've discovered that before he disappeared, Professor Collonges had an extension built at the back of his house. Sloppy job. Done on the cheap. I found an invoice for the work tucked away in his desk. Your name appears at the top of that invoice. How do you explain that, Mr Bilt?'

'Like this,' says the builder, and he presses the red button.

'No,' cried Ralph, jumping back.

'What's the matter?' asked Tom.

'Jack's zapped the Inspector.'

Tom muscled him aside, then shook his head, puzzled. 'No. The copper's still there.'

'*What?*' Ralph squinted again.

The plumber wasn't wrong. Inspector Bone hadn't joined the Lilliput brigade. He could still be measured in metres, not millis. 'It's not worked,' Ralph said. 'Something's gone wrong. Jack looks scared. He's going to the kitchen.'

'I wonder what *that* could be for,' Tom muttered, knowing full well that Jack would probably be searching in his fridge for the stone.

'Bang the glass! Bang the glass! Inspector Bone's coming!'

But there was no need for anyone to make another sound. A second later, the skirt of plastic was lifted and the moustachioed face of Bone peered in.

For one dreadful moment, Ralph feared the policeman might faint with shock. His watercolour eyes froze dead in their sockets when he saw the house and the smoking tree and the dozen or so human beans jumping and waving. Confusion passed over him, then stunned disbelief, then the cold, hard light of understanding. He pushed back the sheet, pushed up his sleeve and craned a hand over the wall of the tank.

Tom grabbed Ralph's shoulders and twisted the boy to face him. 'I'm going back for your mum and Jemima. Climb onto his fingers. Get out while you can.'

But despite these heroic words, the fingers never came. As the hand descended, a resounding *bong* rippled through the air. The hand snaked upwards and out again. Inspector Bone crumpled in a heap on the floor.

And there stood Jack, proudly swinging a far less subtle kind of particle displacer: a wide-bottomed, long-handled frying pan.

Ultimatum

Ralph watched with a kind of helpless fascination as Jack dragged the detective's unconscious body into the space behind *The Frisker*, where he tied him up with a length of washing line and gagged him with a pair of rolled-up socks. And when this ghastly deed was done, Jack slid his bony hands together, stared down briefly at the object of his crime, then turned on his heels and marched towards the tank.

'Everyone, to the house now,' yelled Tom. He grabbed Ralph's arm and yanked him up the steps. 'Hide yourself away. This looks like trouble.'

'What do you think he's going to do?' Wally said as they streamed into the parlour, looking back towards Jack.

They didn't have long to wait for an answer. With a deep-lying structural groan, the whole house was suddenly tilted backwards, then tipped as far the other way, then backwards again. Ralph fell to the floor and collided with a chair as it tumbled over and bowled towards the fireplace. There were frightened cries from all around the room. Neville was hit by a flying painting and Kyle Salter was spilt out through a window. From her ghost-world, Miriam wailed in anger and Ralph thought he heard calls from the tower room as well. What must it be like to be fastened in chains and thrown around like this? he wondered.

With a bump, the house came upright once more and Jack's whispering voice floated through the rooms.

'What's he saying?' Tom shouted, getting back to his feet, clutching his arm just below the elbow. It was bleeding. There was broken glass at his feet.

Ralph strained his ears. The howling wind of Jack Bilt's words had a cruel but definite rhythmic twist. 'I think he's saying…I'll huff and I'll puff and I'll blow your house down.'

Miniville creaked and rattled its bones. And then from the wolf's mouth came a short word, an easy, one syllable, soft-sounding word, that no one, especially not Ralph, could miss. 'Boy…'

'That's you,' said Kyle, lurching in through the door with cinder burns on his face and hands. Behind him, the dying tree still crackled. 'He wants you, Rafe. He wants the little worm who stole his stone. I say we give you up.'

But once again, Kyle's threats could not be played out. After one more stride, he was thrown off his feet as the house rocked again, and this time, ended up flat on its back. Kyle crashed into what had been the ceiling once, breaking a hole in the lath and plaster. Ralph was more fortunate. He'd nearly plunged into the deep fireplace, but had rolled aside and clung to an old wall light. While he lay there, catching his breath, he stared through skylights that used to be windows. Something was coming down through one.

A pair of tweezers.

Agh!

He screamed and rolled away just in time. The points of the tweezers crashed through the window, showering glass like frost being brushed off a privet hedge. The points nipped and clicked, crushing one wall light between their jaws. Tom Jenks, who'd been trapped behind a sliding sideboard, pushed it away and hobbled over, shielding Ralph to the hallway door, now a long hole in the new 'first floor'.

'I've got to go to Mum. She might be hurt,' Ralph panted.

Tom nodded and looked down into the hole. The tiled hall floor was now a vertical drop. The broken stairs curved away to their right. At the far end, at the bottom, was the miniones' room, where they had left Jemima and Penny. 'We'll have to jump for the stairs and grab the newel post,' he said. 'I'll go first, then I'll call you down and catch you.'

Without hesitation, he sat on the wall, dangling his legs through the doorway a second. When he dropped, he hit the post with a thumping clout that would have knocked any lesser man sideways. Not him. Not Tom Jenks.

'OK,' he shouted. 'Come on, you'll be safe.' He stretched an arm, beckoning Ralph down.

It was an image that would haunt Ralph for many days to come. As he steadied himself to make the jump, a thud on the 'ceiling' turned his head. A large bulge had appeared in the area of wall between the two windows. Another thump followed. A shower of plaster fell.

'Ralph, jump!' Tom shouted. But by then it was too late.

With a clatter of bricks and dust and mortar, the point of the tweezers crashed through the wall. Most of the masonry flew through the doorway, showering Tom in an avalanche of rubble, taking him down the stairway with it.

He never had a chance.

Ralph screamed and screamed, and though Neville Gibbons was able to reach him and did his best to hold the boy down, the tweezers, when they came, were far too strong for a mini-man's muscles. They picked Ralph up by the seat of his pants and hauled him out of the broken house. His sweatshirt tore in Neville's hands. His comb fell back through the gaping hole.

Upwards he sailed. Miniville, punctured, wrecked and on its back, was suddenly very tiny below him, then rapidly growing larger again as Jack dropped him onto a castellation above the tower room. Ralph scrabbled to his feet. The castellation was only a few feet wide. It was slippery with moss and pigeon droppings, and felt eager to break at any moment. Ralph knew if he stepped too far to either side he faced a suicidal drop. Forwards, he could walk down the front of the house and jump in through any open window. But forwards was Jack, with a pea-shooter at the ready.

The builder's voice echoed down the barrel. 'Where is it, tyke?'

'Where's what?' yelled Ralph, standing on tiptoes to shout down the barrel.

'The stone you thieved.'

Ralph shook his head.

Jack frowned darkly and drew back the shooter. He loaded a pea and billowed his cheeks.

'No!' Ralph cried out, and covered himself with orang-utan arms.

Zing! The pea shot out and hit the next castellation along. A zig-zagged crack appeared on its surface. With a groan, the larger part broke away, shattering against the aquarium floor with a distant, ugly snap.

Jack trained the shooter back on his victim.

'I hid it,' Ralph shouted. 'It's under the floorboards.' A lie, of course, but he was stalling for time.

Jack clicked the tweezers hard. 'Find it or I'll squish you up.'

Ralph gulped and spread his hands. 'You knocked the house over. The stone will have moved.'

Jack drew back, twitching his lip.

Got you, Ralph thought, and lied again: 'It might take ages to find.'

The builder loaded another pea.

'If you shoot me, Tom will crush it,' Ralph wailed. 'Then what will you do?' He ducked as the pea whistled past his ear. It pinged against the far wall of the aquarium.

'I'll recharge this one,' Jack said quietly. He turned his arm. From a cradle on the underside of his wrist, he unclipped a stone the same size and shape as the one from the fridge. It was grey and lifeless. Dead.

'So, is the stone I took fully charged?' Ralph asked.

The question seemed to annoy Jack immensely. 'Just

get it,' he boomed. 'You've got one hour. Or I'll turn you into water babies.'

'Water?' Ralph shouted, not sure he'd heard right.

Jack laughed out loud and stabbed the tweezers through the house wall again, making a hole even bigger than the first. The shockwave brought Ralph down to his knees. Somehow, he managed to hold his pitch.

'Change of plan,' the builder snarled. 'Going to turn the house into a sunken castle.'

'Castle?' Ralph said, straining to hear. It was difficult to understand the longer sentences.

'New attraction,' Jack said. 'Welcome to *The Shredder.*' From his pocket he pulled out a polythene bag. It was bulbous with water. Two long, finned creatures were swimming around inside it.

Piranha fish.

'You're crazy,' said Ralph, watching the piranhas jazzing back and forth, prodding their irate noses to the polythene.

'Home time,' Jack said snidely. He punched out the nearest window, then clamped the tweezers to the seat of Ralph's pants and unceremoniously dropped him through it.

Immediately, Miniville was righted again. Ralph rolled like a piece of tumbleweed and was only halted when his body collided with a moving snake of metal. Chains. He must be in the tower room. He blinked and looked up. A wild-haired, bearded man stared back.

'You!' gasped Ralph.

'Twenty-first letter of the alphabet,' said the man. 'Comes between 't' and 'v', fiddle dee!'

Ralph slapped a hand across his forehead. Of course, how could he have been so thick? He should have guessed all along who was in the tower room. The man who had probably been the very first minione: the missing genius, Ambrose Collonges.

Delta Theta

Until that moment, Ralph had always imagined that towering genius would be matched by height. But even with regard to his miniaturised state, the professor would have stood little taller than the average post box. Fidgety and nervous, he eyed Ralph suspiciously, a task not made particularly easy by a serious tic below one eye. The skin there was twitching like a rabbit's nose. Ralph stuck it for a second then had to look away, fearful of some kind of strobe effect.

From a shirt pocket stained by yellow chalk dust, Ambrose Collonges pulled out a pair of unruly spectacles and wired them around his cup-handle ears. He leant forward, pupils splashing wide open, eyes the colour of wetted slates. 'A boy. What joy. Another toy for Jack.'

Now it was Ralph's turn to back away in fear. 'Please. Don't hurt me. I k-know who you are. I'm not your enemy. My name's R-Ralph.'

'R-Ralph!' Collonges barked. '*Ralph! Ralph! Rrr-alph!*' Scratching his ear like a flea-bitten squirrel, he approached with a half-maniacal leer, not so much a scientist as a mad scientist's assistant (the one who was always called 'Igor' in the movies).

Thump. Ralph found himself up against a heavy wooden door, similar in size and thickness and shape to the one they'd stopped by on the landing of the house. He rocked the handle. It was firmly locked. No key. No escape from the mad professor. Collonges stretched out his hairy hands, raising his chains to the level of Ralph's neck. Calamity. The Frankenstein monster had been unleashed and the innocent victim had nowhere to run.

But just then, the air between them shimmered and Miriam, the dainty Miriam, appeared. The professor immediately shrank into a corner, the shackles rattling against his bones.

Miriam put her hands on her hips and frowned. 'You see, Rafe? You see what a dreadful tangle he makes?' She pointed to an overturned writing desk, a broken chair, a full-sized matchbox (presumably a bed), an upset bucket of human waste and a couple of half-eaten hundreds and thousands.

'The ghost! The ghost!' Collonges wailed.

'Oh, boo!' went Miriam, to shut him up.

The professor jumped like a wounded gazelle, worrying his hands underneath his chin in the way that a hamster might bunch its paws.

'Miriam, you've got to get me out of here,' said Ralph. Two minutes of his hour were already up. And his mum would be going frantic with worry. He thought about shouting out to her or Tom (*Tom: was he alive or not?*), but even if they'd heard him, could they get him out?

Miriam, meanwhile, swished towards a wall. 'Look here, Rafe. What did I tell you? Wiggly, squiggly scribbles, all over.'

Ralph had noticed the writing on the walls and was faintly curious to know what it meant. Steering well clear of the terrified prisoner, he crunched through some pieces of shattered window pane to investigate the doodles a little more closely. They were chalked up in every available space, like hieroglyphics on a mummy's tomb. Complex scientific equations. Ralph recognised some letters from the Greek alphabet and one or two familiar mathematical symbols, but a monkey might just as well have written the maths for all the sense it made to him.

'All day,' Miriam chuntered. 'Rattle, scribble; scribble, rattle. It's enough to drive a girl to bubbly, Rafe.' And from some everlasting cupboard of ghostly props she produced a long-stemmed, fluted glass and sipped what appeared to be champagne from it.

Ralph looked at the equations again and this time

noticed something unusual. There was a pattern to them. They weren't the random squiggles that Miriam seemed to think: a whole block was repeated over and over. He circled one example with a piece of chalk. 'What does this mean, Professor?'

Collonges lifted the flap of his shirt and scratched at his sore-skinned, bag o'bones ribs. 'Particle redistribution,' he babbled, 'reversible functions. Converging parameters. Counter iterations. Delta theta.'

In the car-boot sale of dumb brain cells, Ralph suddenly had a major clearout. Delta theta. *That's* what the old man had been wailing all this time. Not 'Belt the Keeper' or 'Melt the heater'. *Delta theta.* But what could it mean?

He stepped nearer. Collonges twitched his chains. 'It's OK, I just want to talk,' Ralph said. 'I know about transgeneration. I read in the paper how you proved your theories by moving a potato from one plate to another.'

Collonges nodded, his eyes almost bouncing off the inside of his specs. In a voice full of fearful memories he said, 'A spud. A spud. He was up to no good.'

'You mean Jack?'

'Jack! Jack! Stabbed me in the back!'

'He saw you, didn't he? That's what happened. He sneaked into your laboratory and watched the tests. Then he stole the watch. Didn't he?'

The professor beat his fists against his knees. 'Into the dog bowl, whole,' he wailed.

'And then threatened to feed you alive to Knocker? If you didn't teach him how to use it?'

Collonges let out a high-pitched moan. In the rafters above him, something stirred. Ralph shuddered and raised his gaze. The sloping beams were alive with bats. Bats. Oh, good. This house got better all the time.

'Why is he keeping you in chains?' he pressed. And how had Jack managed that, anyway? he wondered. The chains were bolted firmly to the wall. It would have been impossible for Jack's big hands to shackle the professor after he'd been miniaturised. So was he chained to the wall before he was zapped? Had Jack taken him to the house in Yorkshire? Had they gone there together as business partners, where Jack had done the dirty on him?

The tic began to drive Collonges' eye again. Something wasn't right here, Ralph decided. But for now he let it pass. In fifty-five minutes' time, it wouldn't matter who was misleading who: piranhas weren't fussy who they ate.

'Professor, I've something to show you,' he said and closed his hand around the stone in his pocket.

'Rafe, the ogre's watching,' said Miriam.

Ralph glanced through the broken window. The great round eye of the magnifying glass was trained on the tower room. If Jack saw the stone, that would be that. 'Miriam, have you got curtains?'

'Why, yes,' she said and turning into vapour, she whooshed into the rafters, displacing all the bats. They took flight in one gigantic flock.

'Miriam!' Ralph complained, flapping and ducking and falling to his knees. Next time Mr Gifford, his Drama teacher, asked him to imagine how a teaspoon felt in a mug of swirling tea leaves, he would be able to draw upon the perfect life experience. He covered his ears to block out the squeals the bats were emitting and prayed they wouldn't land on him and suck his veins dry (or worse, turn into a vampire army).

The first *thunk-thunk* erased that fear. Glancing up, he saw the bats clustering in the bay, settling flat against the window panes, shutting out the light and even covering up the holes. They were forming a living quilt. Curtains.

Ducking as the last bat strafed his collar, Ralph turned quickly to Ambrose Collonges. 'What does this do?' He pulled out the stone.

'Oh, Rafe,' cried Miriam, as the stone sent out a pulse of light and she had to disappear to dodge being zapped.

A sticky trail of frothy saliva trickled off Professor Collonges' lips. The tic below his eye slowed down, then stopped, and he was at Ralph's shoulder in a bow-legged stride. He snatched up the stone and held it to his eye.

'I found it in Jack's fridge,' Ralph said, slightly concerned that the old man had mugged him. He tried (politely) to take the stone back, but Collonges buried it inside his shirt as if he were protecting a week-old kitten. Its hard rays splintered the loose-knit cotton, lending him a kind of electrified look.

'Can we use it?' Ralph asked. 'It did something to Miriam—'

'Rafe, you're such a cad,' came her disembodied voice.

'If I don't give it back to Jack in an hour, he's going to drown us. Do you understand?'

Collonges ground his teeth. His eyes slewed sideways towards the wall. He touched a finger to the boxed equation, pressing so hard that his knuckle cracked. 'Coat hanger,' he hissed.

'Pardon?' said Ralph.

'Coat hanger,' Collonges snapped, making a spiralling upward movement.

Ralph thought about this. 'Like an aerial, you mean?'

The professor squeaked and did a little shuffle.

Ralph responded with a long, slow nod. 'Anything else?'

'Mirrors!' said Collonges, glaring at him wildly.

Ralph chewed his lip. 'My mum's got a mirror – in her bag.'

Collonges batted his fists in excitement. 'Wire,' he snorted.

'Easy,' said Ralph. He'd seen a large reel of it somewhere in the house.

'Lenses,' Collonges challenged him loudly.

'You're wearing them,' said Ralph. He pointed to the specs.

The old man jumped as if a nettle had stung him. 'A box! A box! For ten bundles of socks!'

Ralph bracketed his hands about a foot apart. 'About this big?'

The professor's eyes bulged with triumph and delight.

Ralph turned a half-circle and shouted to the rafters. 'Miriam, where are you?'

'I'm not coming out till you put that thing away!'

'Miriam, I *need* you.'

'Here, dahling,' she said, manifesting at his side in a flash.

Ralph pointed to the door. 'You've got to get me out of here.'

'But Rafe, this is the best room in the house. It captures the sunlight in the afternoons.'

'Miriam, please, this is important. Walk through the door and go and find my mum. Tell her I'm here. Tell Neville he's got to break the doors down.'

'Oh Rafe, don't be such a ruffian,' she said. 'Use the key, like everyone else.'

'There's a key?'

Miriam raised the mat. There on the floor was a large, old-fashioned key. Ralph gritted his teeth. What was that line that actors always used: 'Never work with children or animals'? Someone ought to add 'ghosts' to the list.

He snatched the key up and opened the door. Within seconds, he was pounding down a spiralling flight of steps to unlock the second door out to the landing. He shouldered it open, bursting through, covered in cobwebs and spiders. The sound brought several miniones running. Among them were Penny and Neville Gibbons.

'Oh Ralph,' Penny cried. 'We thought he'd killed you.' She swept him madly into her arms. She was shaking and Ralph could taste blood on her neck. He didn't like to think about what she'd been through. Even so, he squeezed himself clear.

'Mum, let me go. We don't have much time.' He touched her face to comfort her. With her jeans badly ripped and her hair exploding out of her clip, she looked like a wild-eyed cavewoman. 'Jack's given us an hour to find the stone. If we don't give it back to him, he'll flood the tank.'

'Have you lost it?' she asked, looking frightened.

Ralph shook his head. 'The professor's got it.'

Neville squinted up the stairs. In the mayhem, he'd lost his glasses. Without them, he looked rather child-like and vulnerable. 'Is that him, in t'chains? Chap who made t'transgenerator?'

Ralph nodded. 'Jack's been holding him prisoner. He'll save us. I know he will. All he needs is some wire and a mirror and a coat hanger and—'

'What for?' asked Penny, cutting him off.

Ralph stared at his mum with a physicist's eye. 'We're going to build a new device,' he said.

Betrayal

'To do what?' said a voice.

Ralph whipped around. Kyle Salter was standing at the back of the group. He banged a spear against the landing and the miniones parted to let him through. Stripped to the waist like a Navajo brave, the bully had never looked quite so scary. On his head and chest were lines of warpaint, drawn from a mixture of blood and charcoal. In his eyes was a hungry desire for combat.

'You *gave* the stone away?'

Ralph felt his knees buckle. 'Where's Tom?' he begged his mum.

'Dead,' said Kyle.

Penny wheeled on him. 'He is *not*. Don't *say* that.'

'Good as,' sneered Salter. 'He's broken. Useless. He's in the next room, laid out like a stiff. Wally's done his back in, Spud's as bad, and Nev needs a guide dog without his specs. I'm in charge now, *Rafe*.'

'Over my dead body,' growled Penny. 'You're going to listen to Ralph and listen carefully. He hasn't once been wrong about Jack or this house. Your swaggering won't set us free, Kyle Salter, but this professor might. It makes sense to give the stone to the one person who'll know what to do with it. So get down off your high horse and start searching for the things Ralph needs for this device. What were they again, Ralph, so we all know?'

She planted her feet and put her hands on her hips. Ralph sighed and rattled off the list.

'Well?' Penny said, giving Kyle the eye.

'I repeat,' he snarled, using his height to intimidate her. 'What's this gadget gonna do?'

'Return us to full size, we hope,' said Wally, pulling Kyle round to face him. 'Then Jack's yours. We all agreed, people?'

The group nodded.

Jemima, standing next to Wally, shuddered.

Kyle sloped his spear and looked around the faces before coming back to poke Wally's shoulder. 'I wanna be the first one big again, deal?'

'Deal,' said Wally, without taking a vote.

Neville sighed. He took a hammer and a cold chisel out of his belt. 'I'd best get upstairs and set this chap free. Ralph, come and do the introductions, will thee? The rest of you mend your wounds – and start searching for these components, fast.'

As the group dispersed, Ralph whispered to his mum, 'I want to see Tom.'

'No,' she said quietly, clasping his hand. 'He's very poorly. The quickest way to help him is to overcome Jack. Go with Neville. I'll stay with Tom.' And she kissed him once and told him she loved him. And for once, Ralph was comforted to hear it.

Over the next fifteen minutes, all manner of bits and bobs were delivered to the table in the tower room. This was Wally's suggestion to the miniones: bring anything you can find that might be used in some kind of electrical gadget. He privately agreed with Ralph that the stone was some form of alien metal, a bit like the legendary dilithium crystals that drove the engines of the *Starship Enterprise*. It was clearly capable of destabilising force fields. You didn't need the brain of a super-computer to guess that Professor Collonges was planning to construct a device that could tune into the wavelengths of the bipolar transgenerator and somehow scramble or reverse its functions. But could this be achieved by cobbling together coat hangers, hair grips, thimbles, clothes pegs, tin foil, bottle tops, mirrors, coins, the motor from Neville's clapped out razor and the entire contents of Wally's electrical kit? Mrs Spink had even brought a tasselled cushion – for the professor to sit on, she claimed.

Ambrose Collonges seemed to think so. He rummaged and clawed through the heap of rammel, throwing away anything he didn't need and barking out requests for anything he did. There were plenty of tools to hand, and it wasn't long before the smell of melting solder was charring the air and fizzing blue sparks were perforating the shadows in the tower room. Ralph had never seen genius like it. One of his favourite TV programmes was a thing called *Scrapyard Challenge*, in which teams of people were given the task of building a rocket, say, from the pieces of scrap they found around the yard. This was the same, in a scaled-down version. At first, it seemed impossible that anything useful could be made from the gubbins Professor Collonges was winnowing through, but the object that eventually came together, though looking deceptively simple, was, in actuality, impressively scientific.

It was not unlike a kitchen juicer (its body was a plastic measuring jug): round, with a funnel-shaped extension on top. Inside, through the curved transparent walls, wires twisted in pasta-shaped spirals, and mirrors trapped and bounced the light. The rod of Tom's belt buckle swung back and forth, acting as a switch of some kind between two carefully-bent paper clips. A coat hanger aerial wagged and trembled. And in the funnel extension, a circle of hair grips was arranged in an overlapping, criss-crossing cradle, into which the professor now fitted the stone.

The insides of the jug turned silver-blue.

Ralph caught his breath. 'Is it done?' he asked. He checked his watch. Two minutes left. Salvation, just in time.

The professor stood back, grinning like a haddock. 'Iterations, iterations, iterations...' he muttered.

Ralph flagged a hand. 'Shall I call the others?'

Ambrose Collonges slewed his eyes sideways. 'Door,' he hissed. He made locking gestures.

Ralph shrugged in confusion. Why would he do that? Why would he want to lock them in again?

Collonges gathered the device into his arms and carried it further across the room.

'What does it do?' Ralph asked. He was beginning to feel just a little uneasy about the professor's selfish behaviour. He didn't seem grateful for the help they'd given him. He hadn't even said thank you for being unchained. And he certainly wasn't acting like a man whose first interest was the liberation of his fellow prisoners. Ralph took a step forward. 'Show me how it works.'

'Back! Back! Or I'll turn your eyes black!'

Ralph jumped back automatically. But was he suspicious or was he frightened? He couldn't pin the feeling down. 'Is it dangerous?' he asked. For now he came to think about it, surely it had taken years in the lab for Collonges to develop the device on Jack's wrist? This do-it-yourself-in-under-sixty-minutes version was completely untested. How many potatoes had exploded or atomised before the boffin had got the technology right?

Too late to be thinking that now. Collonges prodded a switch, made from a toggle off Mrs Spink's cardigan. The gadget sent out a high-pitched whine. To Ralph's amazement, a vortex of green light began to fan out from the tip of the aerial. The bats that were covering the windows screeched. Quickly, they took to the air again, fleeing through the ragged holes in the glass or sluicing away down the well of the stairs. Ralph heard shouts from the body of the house and knew there'd be a crowd in here once the bats had cleared.

'What's happening?' he cried, cupping his ears to shut out the hum.

The professor licked his nose with the tip of his tongue in the manner of a man who was concentrating *deeply*. He twiddled two knobs made from plastic bottle tops and levered a clothes peg on the device, directing its signal out into the lounge. 'Delta theta,' he cackled.

Ralph peered into the lounge. There stood a perplexed-looking Jack, checking the settings on the transgenerator watch. The green pyramid was blinking rapidly. He tapped it, then twisted it left and right. The professor let out an evil laugh. His new device hummed and bobbled about the table. A ball of light bounced from mirror to mirror. From somewhere within it came a warning beep.

'The red! The red! To be in my bed!' Collonges tweaked the knobs again and the green light crackling out of the aerial turned a particular shade of red.

On Jack Bilt's wrist, the same-coloured pyramid began to blink…

'Don't move that clothes peg!' Ralph cried out. At last, he'd worked out what was going to happen. *Touch the red and you'll be in my bed.* He meant his matchbox bed, here in Miniville. The professor had no intention of restoring the miniones back to full size, he was out to gain his revenge on Jack – by swapping places with him.

Ralph lunged towards the table. He grabbed the device and turned away with it, shielding it from the professor's grasp. But as he fiddled with buttons and catches and pegs, anything that might be an on-off switch, his foot located a rolling pin (how *that* could have been used in an electrical gizmo was anybody's guess) and he crashed to the floor, holding the device in the well of his chest.

Collonges was over him, roaring like a bear. The Frankenstein hands came forward again and were on Ralph's neck as he screamed for help.

Schwuup! A spear flashed through the air, striking Collonges hard in the shoulder. He yelped like a puppy and slumped to one side. At the same time, the space above them shimmered and Miriam tried to come to Ralph's aid. But the strange device had not been deactivated, merely retargeted. There was a pop, followed by an intense flash of light and Miriam's form went whooshing through the ether, as if she'd been accelerated to 'warp factor nine'.

Kyle Salter and Neville pounded forward. Kyle pulled the spear from Collonges' shoulder. With the flat of his foot, he pushed the professor away from Ralph. 'Tie him up,' he said to Neville, and to Ralph: 'Get up.'

Ralph struggled to his feet.

Kyle yanked him forwards by the hair. 'So, you've never been wrong about anything, eh, mummy's boy?'

'Get off, Salter. I stopped him escaping.'

'No,' said Kyle, 'we did that.' He shook his spear tip under Ralph's nose so the boy could smell the scent of blood. Then his gaze fell on the device. 'Nice toy,' he said and snatched it up. At last, Kyle Salter had what he wanted: command of the group and the power of the stone.

His triumph, however, lasted all of three seconds. First, Knocker gave out a warning howl. Then a meteor crashed into the side of the tank.

That was what it felt like, at any rate – some spinning object impacting unstoppably with the world as the miniones knew it. The boom alone was almost enough to shake the house to rubble. For several seconds there was utter confusion. Shoving Ralph aside, Kyle started yelling orders, thinking Jack had taken a hammer to the house.

Then Neville reported, 'No, it were a plate. It flew into the tank wall and smashed to smithereens.'

'A plate?' said Ralph.

Neville rubbed his eyes. 'Aye – oh 'eck, look out!' He ducked as a dog bone flew towards them and ricocheted off the trestle table.

'What's going on?' Kyle shouted at Ralph.

Typical. As if Ralph knew the answer.

But, as usual, he was the first to work it out. A hurricane was whistling through Annie's house. Dozens of objects were lifting off their resting places and flying at great speed around the lounge. Air traffic control was non-existent. Ralph knew straight away there was only one force capable of producing such activity. A ghost. A very unstable ghost.

Miriam was out of Miniville – and how.

Jack Attack

Terrible forces, Ralph remembered her saying. Terrible forces would be unleashed if she went outside her place of haunting. The fabric of the universe would be disrupted, space would fold and a black hole would form in Annie's front room. Well, maybe it wouldn't be quite *that* bad, but there was certainly no doubting the physical evidence of Miriam's distress. Her spirit was well and truly 'troubled' as Mrs Spink might say, and the extent of the trouble could be proportionately measured in flying tea mugs.

Ralph almost felt sorry for Jack. The builder never knew what hit him – literally. Stuff was winging in from all directions. It wasn't just the cushions and the mugs in the lounge. The entire small, movable contents of the kitchen were being gathered into the growing whirlwind. The first thing to hit him was a copper-bottomed saucepan. It pranged off his pigeon chest, knocking him backwards, towards the sofa. He twirled and fell onto it, but the cushions just as quickly ejected him, sending him sprawling back into the ring, where a soup ladle dinked off his lanky-haired head and a fork buried its prongs into his thigh.

Justice. Of a sort.

Under normal circumstances, the miniones would have been leaping for joy to see their captor so tormented and humiliated. But no one in the house spared a thought for rejoicing, for they were in terrible danger, too. Although Miriam's destructive brouhaha seemed to be directed exclusively at Jack, anything within its range was fair game. Several times, the Miniville aquarium had shuffled alarmingly across the trestle table. If it was sucked up and thrown across the room there were going to be serious casualties. And if it wasn't thrown, how long would it be before it fell off the table and dashed itself against the floorboards, anyway? And if it wasn't dashed, how long could the tiny house survive without being crushed by some flying object?

Like Knocker's wooden leg, for instance?

Ralph had seen the malformed terrier go running for the space at the back of the sofa. But, in the middle of the floor, the mutt had been clonked by a flying ashtray. Dizzied and confused, he'd fallen over and rolled onto his back. The cyclone had pulled him through a half-circle, tugging at his spindly, upturned legs as if they were dandelions caught in a twister. The broom handle leg, ticking back and forth with all the fury of a crazed metronome, had quickly worked itself free of the elastic that held it to the stump of Knocker's shrivelled limb. Then it was up and in the current. It shot to the ceiling, taking out the light bulb on its way, before rattling along a section of the cornice and dropping tamely into the tank. It landed, end on, centimetres from the east wing of the house. The boom was horrendous, the quake terrifying. Every brick in Miniville readjusted its mortar packing. On the base of the tank, a frosted white star of cracks and fractures radiated out from the point of impact. For half a second, the leg stood upright, then fell. Had it fallen against the roof of the house what hope would there have been for the miniones inside? But it didn't hit the roof, it keeled towards the tank wall, lodging itself against a top corner.

A lucky escape – in more ways than one.

Neville was the first to realise it. He ran to the window and boldly peered out. 'We can climb it,' he said. 'We can climb Knocker's leg.'

'Neville, get down!' Ralph screamed. The fingernails jar had just gone up and the clippings were being sucked out and sprayed around the lounge. Jack took fifty in the head and chest. Dozens more whipped across the face of the tank, raining in at machine-gun speed through the broken, tower-room windows.

'Agh!' cried Neville, strafed by a row across the back of his neck.

'Agh!' went Kyle, paying the price for his arrogant striptease as nails ripped across his naked chest. 'Do something, Perfect. How do we stop this?'

'We can't,' Ralph shouted, sheltering behind the overturned table. 'Not until Miriam calms down.'

That wasn't good enough for Kyle. Ignoring his bleeding wounds, he grabbed Professor Collonges by the collar and pulled the old man into a nose-to-nose face-off. 'Show me how to use this thing you've made. Tell me how to zap the ghost or I'll throw you out the windows before she does.'

The professor blew a raspberry into his face.

Salter bundled him aside and picked up the gadget. He shook it. Nothing happened. He pushed the button. Nothing happened. He pulled the peg. Nothing happened. He twisted the stone inside its hairpins. Nothing happ— no, the gadget buzzed. He tried the stone again.

'Put it down,' yelled Ralph. 'You don't know what you're doing. You might end up swapping places with Jack.'

Why he was giving out such a warning to a boy who'd

bullied him most of his life, Ralph couldn't imagine. But no one in their right mind (and Kyle never had been, in Ralph's opinion) would want to be in Jack's shoes now. The pan Jack had used to fry Inspector Bone (who'd disappeared, Ralph noticed; now where had *he* gone?) was dancing in front of the bewildered builder, beating him backwards towards *The Frisker*. As Jack's body fell between the gross rubber hands, the bulbs came on and flashed with the zest of a winning fruit machine. Then the gloves began to do their work, slapping Jack's head, and only his head, sparring him upright for half a minute till his eyes rolled back and his mouth began to dribble and his melon of a brain must have turned to pulp. He slumped to the floor in a pin-striped heap. And from around the back of *The Frisker* came a hand. A hand showing weal burns at the wrist. It was Bone, somehow free from his clothes-line tangle. He flipped open a pair of cuffs and...

Snap. Jack Bilt was under arrest. Clamped to the long, if shaky-looking, arm of Detective Inspector Nicholas Bone.

'He's got him,' Ralph whooped. 'Bone's nabbed Jack.'

If only Kyle Salter had been paying attention. 'It's working,' he laughed, as a green charge crackled out of the aerial.

'Leave it,' cried Ralph. But his warning was too late. Disaster was about to strike. Though tied, Professor Collonges could kick. He aimed a vicious poke at the back of Kyle's knee. Kyle bucked and lurched forward, spilling the device high into the air. It fizzed and pulsed all the way to its landing, dumphing in the centre of a tasselled cushion.

A flash of green light enveloped the cushion and gave it a radioactive glow.

And then it proceeded to grow.

And grow and grow and grow and grow...

'Out, boys! Now! Before you're crushed!' Neville yelled. And, diving past the cushion, he grabbed Kyle Salter round the waist and dragged him manfully towards the door. With the open stairs behind them, Ralph and Kyle were out of danger. But Professor Collonges was not. As the fabric of the cushion began to press against the walls, stretching to fill all available spaces, the mad inventor was trapped in a corner, unable to escape.

Neville ran forward to attempt a rescue, but could find no way past the growing mound. And so he took a saw from his belt and sliced it, cutting and stabbing in the hope that the woolly balloon would burst or he could chop a hole right through its centre and pull

Professor Collonges clear. The feathers and dust of countless decades spilled into the tiny tower room. But that wasn't all that came out of the cushion. By the time he'd realised what he'd released, Neville Gibbons was completely surrounded. The leading wave was heel-height and growing. The most frightening creatures Ralph had ever seen.

Dust mites.

Battleground Miniville

They had six, sturdy, triple-jointed legs and looked like bleached, translucent beetles. Protruding from their backs was a number of hairs that seemed to Ralph to have little or no function. They did not, for instance, appear to aid balance. For as the mites tumbled out around Neville's feet, they stumbled, directionless, rather than ran, as if the sudden exposure to freedom and light had disrupted their sense of navigation.

'What are they?' asked Kyle, looking terrified and sick. The first to come near him he backed away from. The second he kicked. The third he stamped out. It vanished with a weak, wet splat as if he'd pricked a hole in a flabby plum. All that remained was a flat bag of skin and a dash of red colouring that distinguished the creature's simple mouth parts from the rest of its otherwise colourless body.

'They're mites,' Ralph said. 'We've got to get out of here.' From somewhere in the back of his brain he recalled the frightening statistic that up to half the weight of an old pillow or cushion could be attributed to these normally harmless, microscopic creatures. If the cushion exploded there were going to be thousands of them in the room. Thousands. Growing larger. They had to run.

'Neville, come on,' Ralph shouted out loud, as the carpenter stood there, bewildered and shocked. The mites were swarming around his legs and beginning to scuttle up as high as his knees. Ralph snatched up a piece of wood and swept a small corridor through their ranks, sending dozens of the creatures crashing aside.

'Let's go!' he screamed, tugging Neville's shirt.

'W-what about t'professor?' Neville stammered fearfully, abandoning his saw to the still-swelling cushion. He came back towards the door, beating mites off the hem of his apron, squashing them in his pockets, shaking them out of the turn-ups of his trousers.

Ralph looked towards the corner where the old man had been. It was fat with cushion. The mad professor of particle physics was lost behind the ruin of his own invention. All he could hope for was a pocket of air. And maybe, after his attempt at treachery, that was all he deserved. 'No chance,' Ralph yelled, shaking his head.

'Can you stop them growing bigger?' Neville said, dancing through the horde as the tide grew stronger and a wave of mites peeled away to scale the walls and pour into the chimney breast and scuttle towards the windows. If something wasn't done to block them off soon, they would be all through the house, Ralph realised. He looked towards the corner again. The mites were teeming there already, but through the swelling bubble-pack of fat little bodies, a faint green pulse could still be detected. The device, the cause of so much anguish, was under that heaving mass.

Impulse drove Ralph forward. Brave or stupid? There wasn't time to tell. He simply plunged his hand through the sea of mites in front of him, grabbed the device and yanked it clear. A cloud of mites fell free, but one glued its sticky, hairy legs onto his arm. It was the size of his fist – and *still* growing. Ralph watched it dip its head and remembered, in horror, that creatures such as this fed on the flaked, dead skin of humans. Its mouth parts opened. A thin proboscis emerged. Ralph screamed and smacked his hand against the wall. With a splat, the mite burst. A wet stain made the chalk marks run.

Kyle yanked him through the door, slammed it to and locked it, killing any mites that had scuttled through with them. No one argued as they clattered down the stairs, into the crumbling belly of the house.

On the landing they were met by Wally, running up. 'What's happening? Did it work? Where's the professor?'

'Eaten alive, with any luck,' said Kyle.

Panting, Neville explained the situation. 'We need t'get everyone alerted. There's—'

He broke off, hearing a girl's shrill scream.

'Trouble at t'mill,' said Kyle, filling in.

Together, they dashed into the miniones' room. To Ralph's horror, mites were dropping down the chimney stack and flowing across the open floorboards. Jemima was fixed in a corner with Sam, who was using a scouring pad as a shield to hold the oncoming tide at bay. It was a hopeless task. The creatures, some as large as ankle-height, were dropping through the windows and gaps in the brickwork and using each other as stepping stones to form a bulging, foaming mass. Even Kyle Salter didn't need a calculator to work out that Sam would soon be outnumbered.

'Jem, hold on!' he cried, and dived in amongst the mites, flashing his spear with gladiatorial bravery and pounding his feet like a child let loose in a paddling pool.

In that moment, Ralph learnt three things about Kyle. First, his heart was not as black as he liked to make out. Two, he had a soft spot for Jemima Culvery. Three, he was going to die unless more miniones went to his aid.

Neville ploughed in. So too, Wally.

'Ralph, bring help!' they shouted.

But Ralph was working on a plan of his own. As the house shook again under yet another gale-force pounding from Miriam, as ceilings broke and walls collapsed and plaster and masonry rained down around him, Ralph studied the apparatus in his hands. It was still 'switched on', still faintly humming and the aerial still radiated a pale, green light.

He weighed up the odds. They were not good. In his opinion, the mites were continuing to grow because the device was set, inadvertently, for that purpose. But why hadn't they shot up in size? Was it because the weight of their numbers had stretched the signal far too wide? Or maybe the stone wasn't charged up enough? Or maybe his unevolved, imperfect brain wasn't up to the level of particle physics. He looked at the bottle top dials. If he turned them and the growth rate of the mites increased, the miniones could die a horrible death. Then again, there was an equal chance that the creatures might return to their microscopic state.

Left or right?

Decrease or increase?

Death or life?

He closed his eyes, changed his mind and pulled the

peg instead. The gadget buzzed and Ralph thought he felt an energy surge burst out from it, though what effect it had had he couldn't tell. But when he opened his eyes, the whirling vortex of light from the aerial was wavering towards the same shade of red he had seen in the tower room just before he'd stopped the professor swapping places with Jack.

Suddenly, an idea slapped him in the face. What if…?

'Oi!' Kyle Salter's angry voice retuned Ralph's eardrums to a pitch above soprano. Kyle was at the door, with Jemima (who appeared to have fainted with shock) slung over his shoulder and a dead mite hanging off the end of his spear. Behind him, Neville, Sam and Wally were baiting the mites with pieces of sugar bead, trying to distract them away from the humans.

'Can't hold them!' Neville shouted. 'And…oh, help us. The nearest ones to me are getting bigger.'

Ralph gulped. Was that the surge he'd felt?

'Perfect, move it!' Kyle growled.

Ralph turned immediately to run down the landing, only to see his way blocked off by a mite so large it could have swallowed him whole. His heart thudded. His thighs jellied. The group turned the other way. And there was another bloated beast.

Kyle looked over the banister rail. Some twenty feet

below, the hall was littered with perilous rubble. 'Gonna jump,' he said to Wally. 'Drop Jem to me.' He slid the girl off his shoulder.

'It's suicide,' said Wally, looking aghast. 'You'll break every bone you've got.'

'Got a better plan, have you?' Kyle was saying when the mite nearest Ralph reared up like a horse, kicking and wriggling its short front legs.

To his everlasting shame, Ralph screamed in terror, thinking he was about to be leapt on and consumed. But instead, the creature's flanks began to shrivel and it suddenly imploded like a punctured airship. As it disappeared to nothing but skin and steam, Ralph saw the reason for its termination. Tom Jenks was on the landing, brandishing two torches.

'Heat,' he said, through a badly-cut lip. 'They're just big bags of water, that's all.' He threw a torch to Wally, who promptly dispatched the other large mite and set about forcing the rest of them back.

Ralph hurried to the plumber's side. 'I thought you were dead,' he whispered.

Tom smiled and showed him a large chest bandage. 'Your mum's a good nurse. Come on, she's waiting. We need to regroup in a safe room downstairs.'

But just when it seemed that the group would at last

be united again, another projectile struck the trestle table and this time, the outcome was catastrophic. Miriam was still at her devastating worst and, if anything, was growing more volatile. It was a planter that did the damage. A large, heavy flower pot that should, by rights, have been outside, not in. Annie had always kept it in the bay where her range of green ferns could appreciate the early-afternoon sunlight. The ferns and their earth had been long-since scattered when the pot had fallen over in the first round of mayhem. For a while, it had lain inert, just bumping up against the corner of *The Frisker*. But when Miriam had set that machine in motion the pot had jiggled free to roll where it liked. When it whacked the front leg of the wonky trestle table, the leg bent at the knee and the fish tank slid. It skated off the table at an angle of precisely forty-three degrees. In less than two-tenths of a second, one corner had speared a bare patch of floor and the tank had come to rest the correct way up. Remarkably, not a millimetre of glass was broken.

The same could not be said for the house called Miniville.

The impact with the side of the tank as it slid, then with the bottom as it flattened out, jarred every brick and beam and slate. The tower room crumbled in on itself and the whole of the west wall buckled with the ease of a domino falling, tilting the house into a precarious slant.

Ralph was one of the lucky ones. He escaped the quake with nothing more than brick dust stinging his eyes and a playground gash just below his left knee. In his hands, he still had the professor's device.

The situation was critical. People were screaming in fear and pain. He knew, now, there would be no way to contain the mites. And one more hit from Miriam might be fatal.

So he made his choice. He made it out of bitterness and anger and frustration and love for his mother and pride for the group. He did not consult the adults or stop to think twice. For, in his view, only one option remained. Trawling his memory for every last scrap of information, he recreated the professor's last movements with the device, working the buttons and moving the peg until the vortex of light had built to a blinding shade of red.

'Touch the red pyramid,' he said through his teeth, rocking back and forth and willing Jack to hear him. The only way he could save his mother and his friends – and hopefully (*please, God*) calm Miriam down – was to do what Ambrose Collonges had wished for, and swap places with Jack.

'Touch it. Touch it. *Touch* it!' he yelled.

Whoosh! With that same awful, dragging sensation he'd felt when he'd first arrived in Miniville, his wish was suddenly granted. Skin and bones grew large again and he landed with a thump on the floor of Annie's lounge. Despite being dizzy with nausea, he was able to detect a cold circle of steel around his wrist. He jiggled his arm and felt the weight of his 'hostage'. Yes. He'd done it. He'd made the swap.

'Inspector, it's me,' he panted.

And a voice slurred back, 'Roll up, do.'

Terror clamped Ralph's heart.

He was handcuffed to Jack.

A Surprise Return

For a few seconds, both parties experienced a fuddled kind of truce as they tried to work out how this had come about. Here they were, taking shelter beside *The Frisker*, trying to avoid being hit by flying objects, bound to each other by a cold, steel bracelet. Ralph looked at Jack's wrist and saw straight away that the watch had been removed. Bone must have taken it. So Bone had pressed the pyramid. Therefore, Bone was now in Miniville. Oops. Jack, in turn, still puddled by his pummelling, checked for his watch and gave a shocked start – gone! He glared at the handcuffs and then at Ralph and possibly wondered why it was that policemen looked so much younger these days. Then his grey eyes fell upon the device made of clothes pegs and mirrors and pins, and that fairground organ he laughingly called a brain began to grind out an explanatory tune. '*Meddlesome brat from house next door. Empty fridge. Stolen stone. Contact with Collonges. New device. Escape.*'

His eyes met Ralph's for a nanosecond.

Then the pair of them started to wrestle.

It was a bizarre sight, a grown man of forty and a boy

of twelve grappling for control of a mad professor's miniaturising gadget.

'Gimme that,' snarled Jack, tugging it towards him.

The device buzzed. Ralph pulled it back.

'I'd rather die, Bilt!'

'Git up, Knocker. Nip him!'

Knocker got up, carrying his broom handle fetched from the tank, pathetically in his jaws.

Somewhere out of sight and out of doors, thunder rumbled and a flash of blue lightning gorged the plastic sheets at the windows. Something was coming. Something bad.

'Miriam!' Ralph yelled, wondering why the ghost hadn't come to his aid. She had calmed down suddenly and he sensed she'd left the room. But why?

'Oo's Miriam?' said Jack, sinking his yellow teeth into Ralph's wrist.

'Agh!' the boy screamed and kicked Jack in the crotch.

'Ooh,' went the builder, curling up. He jabbed his elbow into Ralph's chest.

Winded, Ralph nearly let go of the device. It responded with a warning beep.

'Miriam! Miriam! Help me! It's Rafe! Stop the ogre or we're all going to die!'

Another luminescent flash of lightning gripped the room.

And then a woman's voice said, 'Is there anybody there?'

The tug-of-war came to an instant halt. 'Oo's that?' hissed Jack.

Ralph wasn't sure. She was in the hall, just out of sight. There was something very eerie about the way she'd asked the question. She'd used a deep, theatrical tone as if she were an actress rehearsing her lines, performing to the echoes in the auditorium, calling out to the shadows left behind in the seats.

'Don't be afraid. Show yourself,' she said. The words floated through the doorway and hung in the air like a magic spell.

The blue sheets at the windows billowed.

Knocker whined in fear and dropped his wooden leg at Jack's side.

Thunder cracked.

And in the flash which followed, Miriam's body briefly materialised.

'Bloomin' Nora,' Jack said.

This time, the visiting woman heard him.

'Mr Bilt?' she inquired, with a twitter of apology. She tapped faintly at the door but still didn't enter. 'I hope you don't mind, but I let myself in. The spare key is still in the plant pot out front.'

Ralph let out a shocked gasp, hardly able to believe who it was. A pair of elderly, brown-stockinged legs in a pair of elderly, black brogue shoes were just becoming visible when *crack!* something broke against the side of his neck and he sagged forward like an unstuffed teddy.

H-row? went Knocker as that half of his leg that was not in Jack's hand went spinning over the back of the sofa.

'Fetch,' Jack said, cruelly pushing the terrier aside.

Knocker snapped his teeth and tried to bite, but the movement only unbalanced him again and he rolled over in a sad, lopsided heap, just as Annie Birdlees stepped into full view.

She brought a cross on a silver chain up to her mouth and tottered through the room, looking horrified. 'Mr Bilt. Goodness me. What's happening here? I sensed a troubled presence the moment I arrived and…oh, why is Ralph in a set of handcuffs?'

Jack showed her his best banana-mouthed grin. 'Citizen's arrest. Boy's a menace. Broke in through the cellar. Attacked the dog. Rizzled up a spook and did for the furnishings. Tried to steal me gadget—' He moved the device from Ralph's lap to his, then paused, as something squished in his pocket. '—and me dead prannies. Had no choice but to knock him out and take back what's legally mine.'

Annie shook her head in disbelief. 'No, not Ralph.'

'He's a villain,' said Jack. 'Wants locking up.' He tugged at the handcuffs. 'Can't be *nmph* trusted.'

'That's ridiculous. I shall go to his mother this instant.'

'Wouldn't bother,' said Jack. 'Ran away with a plumber. Terrible business. Turned the boy to crime.'

'Poppycock!' Mrs Birdlees said. 'There's something quite sinister going on in this house and— oh...' With a hand across her breast she knelt down slowly and picked up the open fingernail jar, sighing as she tipped out a solitary clipping. 'My nails,' she said. 'What happened to my nails?'

'They're *yours?*' said Jack, looking rather stirred.

'I left them in the cellar. That's what I came back for. My nails, my ear wax, my hair and my tummy fluff. I've collected my body parts since I was a child. It's my belief, Mr Bilt, that when I die, every last part of me I've made or grown should go with me into my cardboard coffin, in preparation for my chosen life beyond. And you've scattered me, willy-nilly, over the floor. How can I return as a grizzly bear now?'

Jack Bilt turned a grizzly shade of green. 'You're seriously weird,' he said.

Annie stood up straight. 'I'm calling the police.'

And, as if she'd used her magic tone again, there was a sudden screech of tyres outside. She marched to the window and hauled down a sheet. 'Oh, how strange, they're already here...'

'Bone,' muttered Jack. 'Called the bloomin' cavalry.' He jerked the handcuffs urgently, bringing Ralph round.

''Nnie...' Ralph slurred, spitting out a loose tooth. 'Mum's in dur fij tank. Ged dur box ov Jack.'

But Jack, by now, had realised the gadget was his only hope. He was fiddling with its bottle top knobs when two uniformed policemen burst into the room, followed by a man with bushy eyebrows and a beard that looked like a map of Tasmania. He was wearing a white laboratory coat and reading something off a hand-held meter.

'Bilt?' one policeman boomed.

'There,' Annie said with an old lady flourish.

The policeman jerked a thumb. 'You're nicked, chummy.'

Jack Bilt? Never. He threw his free arm around Ralph's neck, pulling the boy to him, making him gurgle.

The arresting officer stalled.

'Erm, the box he's holding,' the white coat said, checking the meter which was whining uncontrollably. 'It's giving off radionic impulses. Confiscate with extreme care, PC Sparrow.'

The second copper, PC Robbins, moved forward. 'Put the box down, Bilt, and let the boy go. Game's up. You ain't got nowhere to run.'

'Roll up,' said Jack, and wiggled the peg hard.

The coat hanger twanged and a crackle of green light leapt across its points.

The scientist's meter whined off the scale. 'Stand back!' he shouted.

Wise advice. Half a second later, Jack and his hostage had completely disappeared.

Into the Wasteland

That was how it seemed to the blinking eye, at least. Both of them had been miniaturised, of course, and pitched close to the wall of the Miniville aquarium. Ralph could smell the drying marmalade. He could see the shattered house through the cataract of glass, but no sign whatsoever of its occupants. He felt sick and dizzy and anxious for his mum, and his neck was begging for a long, cold compress. But there wasn't time for healing or even time to heave. Jack was on his feet and tugging at him hard.

'C'mon, you toe-rag.'

'I hate you,' said Ralph.

And he kicked and he punched and they wrestled again. But this time, the bout was weak and short-lived. The cuff on Ralph's wrist had been set for a man's arm not a boy's, and as they jostled and tussled and the join became strained, Ralph's hand popped out and he staggered back and fell against the tacky marmalade, gummed to it by the arms and shoulders. Jack, Jack, the lucky black cat, had come away with the device. *Typical*, Ralph thought. He always got the duff end of the Christmas cracker.

'Most grateful,' said the builder, flexing his wrist to bring the feeling back. He kicked a fragment of an egg cup aside. From his pocket he produced a miniature penknife. 'Know what you are? A blooming nuisance. Want to see my knife-throwing act?'

Ralph shook his head. 'Behind you,' he said.

'Ho ho. Three bags full,' Jack sneered.

'Knocker! Git down! Now!' Ralph shouted.

Jack jumped like a firework, then. He turned to see a hot tongue idling towards him. It was dribbling with saliva and it smelt of rotting meat. Knocker rolled a lip and showed his teeth. If only... If *only* he'd slurped straight away and not paused to growl it would have been a ghastly, but fitting, end. Jack, licked up by his own 'best friend', a living Jonah in the whale that was his dog. But that momentary lapse gave the builder time to scarper. He hastened away between Knocker's paws, deep into the shadows beneath the dog's pudgy tummy.

Poor Knocker. If he'd had a good leg to scratch his brain with, he would have done. Instead, he grizzled in confusion and turned a half-circle, allowing Ralph the opportunity to slip out of his sweatshirt and take off after Jack, without fear of becoming a dog's dinner himself. He hurried under Knocker and out the other side.

By now, the floor was springing with the transits of giants, every footfall registering a small explosion. Annie, Ralph noticed, was making for the fish tank. He prayed she'd be in time to save his mum and the others. The three men, meanwhile, were on their knees, picking up pieces of damaged crockery, searching for signs of mini-humans. But in the ghost-ravaged wasteland of broken pottery, it was far too easy for Jack to hide. They would never find him or the device. He could disappear for days behind a skirting board, then restore himself to full size and walk away, untouched.

But it didn't happen like that. Suddenly, Jack scrambled out from under a dessert spoon and came running back towards Ralph, faster than a ferret. His arms and legs were a blur of locomotion and his eyeballs were so far out of their sockets they resembled two light bulbs (of very low wattage). When Ralph saw what Jack was running from, he knew he would need the speed of a racehorse to stand any chance of getting away.

Ants move surprisingly fast. So quickly did they swarm to surround the two humans that even Ralph was terrified. He backed against Jack and they circled together, trapped and outnumbered by a ring of soldier ants.

Ralph knew they would need a miracle to escape. They had no weapons – and what good would they be against armoured exoskeletons and acid sprays, anyway? Jack, Jack, the incompetent prat had dropped the transgenerator in his dash – so there wasn't even hope of turning themselves into a couple of pin-pricks and floating away next time Knocker sneezed.

It was over.

Goodnight.

Roll up, do.

The ant nearest Ralph dipped its cone-shaped head. Its scissor-like jaws opened sideways. Its compound eyes rolled over its prey. Ralph saw its feelers arc. He covered his face. Strangely, his young life didn't flash before him. Instead – and what a blooming time for this – he remembered a fantastic film he'd seen in which a tiny company of British soldiers had fought to defend their post, Rorke's Drift, against a monumental army of Zulu warriors. The soldiers were outnumbered twenty-five to one, but had fought so bravely that the warriors eventually ceased to attack and let the wounded survivors go free.

But fighting bravely was not in Jack's blood.

'Take the boy!' he squealed. 'He's young! He's juicy!'

The ants closed in. Jack gave a scream and was carried away, on the backs of a column of six linked workers.

The nearest remaining ant paused before Ralph. Curling its antennae high into the air, it reached out and stroked the boy on the temples. The touch was electrifying. Ralph sensed another kind of world. A world in which little creatures worked for one another and co-operated readily to live a better life. When he opened his eyes, the ants were gone. Who knows why they had spared his life? Who knows why they took Jack Bilt?

A voice boomed overhead. Ralph looked up and saw a human finger coming towards him.

'Here,' the voice was saying. 'Here.'

A glass thudded down, enclosing Ralph inside it. Paper was carefully pushed under its rim. Ralph climbed on to it and lay down, exhausted.

And there he was happy to stay for a while, hoisted to freedom by ground-to-air tumbler. They handed him to Annie while they carried on searching. She sat on the sofa with the glass on her lap, knuckling a tear from below one eye. Ralph stood up and made semaphore waves. Annie dibbled her fingers back. 'Mum?' he mouthed. 'Did you find Mum?'

Annie pressed her fingertips against her mouth. Her gaze drifted across the room. Ralph turned around to see what she was looking at, but PC Robbins was blocking his view. Suddenly, the copper rocked back on his heels, examining some object he'd picked up off the floor. He tilted it between his finger and thumb. Ralph knew straight away that it had to be the second bipolar transgenerator.

'Be careful!' he yelled, slapping his hands against the tumbler.

But Robbins foolishly squeezed his fingers and a dot of red light winked out of the device.

Oh no, thought Ralph, sensing that familiar wobbling of molecules.

With a crash that set Knocker yapping for England, the tumbler exploded and pieces of glass flew in all directions.

'Oh!' squealed Annie, paddling her feet. Ralph was full-sized again, perched on her lap.

The second copper hurried across. 'Berringford, what's happening?'

The scientist ran a scanning device over Ralph's brain. 'Fascinating. Quite fascinating. He's been returned to normal by a reverse transgenic stimulus. Someone must have used the device.'

'I fink that was me,' PC Robbins said. He pulled a bloodstained hand away from his neck. A piece of glass from the tumbler had lodged below his ear. Split between his thumb and forefinger, were the useless remains of a tiny coat-hanger and peg.

Berringford sucked in through his teeth. 'Well, that's most unfortunate.'

'What does that mean for the others?' asked Annie.

To which Ralph added, 'Where's my mum?'

The scientist squinted at the crushed device. 'That really is most regrettable. Oh well, too bad. PC Sparrow, take the boy away.'

'I'm going nowhere without my mum,' Ralph said.

Berringford pushed his glasses to the bridge of his nose. 'All of them,' he said, nodding at a tumbler on the mantelpiece. It was full of little people. Kyle. Neville. Jemima. Tom. Penny Perfect, in Tom's arms. 'They'll all go together. The dog included. Quarantine. Three months. Keep on searching for Bilt, PC Robbins...'

Epilogue

So there you have it. Something horrible happened. Some *things* horrible happened. Ghastly things.

Appalling.

If you were Ralph, what would be the worst of the adventure, do you think? To be bullied and teased by Kyle Salter? To be miniaturised and cooped up in an arcade exhibit? To sleep on a scouring pad? To have to drink water tainted with dog slobber? To grow scrawny on a diet of hundreds and thousands? To do battle with dust mites and grubby buzzing flies and a mad-mad-mad-mad-bad professor?

Or would it be what happened to Ralph next that would spook you?

Imagine this: being taken to a secret laboratory, deep underground below a moor in Northumberland. You're locked in a room where cameras watch your every move. Even when you're sleeping. Even when...yes, that too. You have plenty to eat and are well looked after, but every day, for three months, scientists hook you up to strange machines that make your head buzz while they record any interesting *changes* in you, scratching out results on rolling charts, in looping graphs, in diverse colours. They put needles in your arms and draw your blood. They take snippets of your hair. They bottle your wee. They monitor your dreams, especially your nightmares.

Is this what aliens do to us, you wonder?

Once a day, for two short hours, you're allowed to see your mother and the man she has fallen deeply in love with. They intend to marry, Tom Jenks and Penny Perfect. Lack of height is not a barrier to human feeling. From this you will have guessed that they are still tiny. All the miniones are, including the unfortunate Detective Inspector Bone (like Ralph, you might feel a little guilty about dragging him into Miniville). Berringford, who heads the scientific inquiry into the strange goings-on in Midfield Crescent, as yet has little hope to offer them. Every day he says to Ralph, 'This is why we need you in the project, dear boy.' The project. He always talks about 'the project'. As if Tom and Penny and Ralph and Knocker are little more than mice being prodded with a stick. 'We need to observe your *metabolism*—' he says (He uses a lot of words ending in 'ism'. None of them give very much away.) '—so we might determine the precise effects that transgeneration has on tissue health and, erm, brain power.' And yet when he says this he always slips a tape measure round Ralph's biceps and notes any increase in muscle size and tone.

Now, why would he do that, do you think? You wouldn't be interested in *muscle tone*, would you? You'd be saying to this scientist, 'I want my mum back. My *whole* mum back. When are you going to make her big again?'

And Berringford would tell you, 'It's not that easy,' and do that irritating thing that gentlemen in white coats do with their spectacles: cough on the lenses then polish them on the end of their tie.

Not easy? Phooey! 'Delta theta!' you'd be shouting. Surely the scientists must know *that*? It's written on the wall in the tower room. 'Talk to Professor Collonges,' you'd urge them. 'He'll know what to do.'

But your reply from Berringford would be suitably ambiguous. He would drum his fingers on his clipboard and say: 'Yes, we've, erm, acquired his notes on particle displacement from his academic files at Oxford. We have also recovered the original transgenerator which Bone took from Jack Bilt's wrist. It's very small, of course, and the *felgate crystal* has lost its charge.' (The felgate crystal; ah, that was the stone.) 'Our specialists are attempting to...reconfigure it. We have also hired the services of an excellent archaeologist to, erm, piece together the vase that the boy Luke Baker was mixed up in. He was damaged, I'm afraid, during the disturbances. We're still missing a small section of his left ear.'

'What about…?'

The professor? Hmm. Now, take a deep breath. Are you surprised when Berringford shakes his head? Collonges was squashed by a cushion full of dust mites. The only thing the scientists recovered was his brain. It lies in a deep freeze in Berringford's laboratory. But no one's going to tell Ralph that, are they?

And what of good, kind neighbour, Annie Birdlees? The dear old lady of lavender and lace, described as gruesome at the front of our story (more on that in a moment). Did *she* go into quarantine? No, not Annie. She was allowed to visit Ralph daily and keep him up to date with what was happening in the Crescent.

'They won't allow me into my house,' she complained. 'Do you know, they put a wheel on that poor maimed dog and took him in, hoping that he'd sniff out Mr Bilt?'

Ralph threw up his hands. 'I told you,' he said to a whirring camera, 'the ants took Jack.' They would have stunned him with their sprays of formic acid and…well, you can probably picture the rest. Ralph knew, as I'm sure you clever ones do, that ants cannot chew or swallow solid food. They squeeze out the juice from their prey and drink it, then throw the dry husk of the body away.

Charming.

'How's Miriam?' Ralph would whisper every day.

Oh yes, Miriam, the feisty ghost. You'd certainly want to know what became of her.

'Pining,' Annie would whisper back. 'She believes you've left her, like her intended. It's her lot, Ralph: to pine away until eternity. She won't be happy until you go back.'

So here we are, back, one snowy morning in February. Three months to the day since the miniones were rescued. Annie's house has been cleared of debris and cigarettes and dark blue sheets and seaside attractions (Ralph inquired of PC Robbins what had happened to *The Frisker* and was told it might be used at their local station). The fifty thousand pounds Jack gave for the house was, wouldn't you know it, counterfeit. So the transaction has been annulled and the keys have been returned to their rightful owner. Number 9 Midfield Crescent is Annie's again.

Is she happy to be home? Yes, she is. A brief spell living with her sister in Totnes has taught the old cuckoo that a life of solitude can have its rewards. But she is not fully alone now, of course. Being a woman who has always had encounters with 'the spirits', she has welcomed Miriam into her home. Ralph, too, has moved in for a spell. While the scientists work to 'reinstate' his mother (and oh how he misses her, every hour of every day) he will live, for now, as a ward to Annie.

So, here's the cosy final scene. Annie makes them both a cup of hot chocolate and they sit in the lounge, with Miriam blowing cool air across Ralph's drink and Annie stroking Knocker's head. It was either the bullet or a dogs' home for him until Annie stepped in and said she would have none of it. Blame not the mutt for the malice of its master. That was her line.

Admirable.

The room feels dreadfully large to Ralph. There is very little in it apart from the seats and the shoes Annie Birdlees was wearing at the time (she broke a heel when Ralph played the genie on her lap and took them off because she couldn't walk in them).

The room, yes. It really is a desert. Even the remains of Annie's ferns were taken to the lab so the soil could be filtered through a fine, dry sieve, just in case Jack had wriggled in among the roots and burrowed out a hide deep down in the earth.

Jack, Jack, still unaccounted for. For this reason, the 'authorities', the men in white shirts and plain black suits who hover in the shadows around the scientists have never been able to 'close the book'. They want the builder in their clutches. They want him pinned to a board like a moth. They want evidence of his 'whereabouts'. And nothing, it seems, is beyond their 'reach'. If Ralph and Annie were to strip away these floorboards or look into the garden a metre beyond the window, they would notice signs of 'excavations'. The colony of ants was quickly captured. Forty thousand were taken back to the lab. All were examined (and eventually released). Neither Jack nor his husk was found among them.

So what *did* become of the builder, Bilt? This is on Ralph's mind as Knocker starts to sniff around Annie's shoes and Annie twitters on about her dolls' house in the attic which she thinks could be converted to a number of flats to comfortably hold a dozen or so mini-people. And Miriam says, 'Rafe, what's the matter with your poodle?' (Though inaccurate, she prefers this description to 'terrier'.) And Knocker growls and backs away from an upturned shoe. Is it the pong that's got to him? Or is he wanting to play a game of fetch? Ralph slides to his knees and takes a look.

And oh, lordy-dordy, pump up your heart. There on the sole of Annie's left shoe is a small, squashed figure. It is not an ant. Ants know to run when the shadow of a human foot falls over them. Look closely. No, no, closer than that. You can *just* see the pin-striped suit, perhaps?

Annie. It was Annie who done for Jack.

Dear sweet...innocent...Annie.

Told you she was gruesome, didn't I?

MORE RED APPLES TO GET
YOUR TEETH INTO . . .

1 84121 456 6   £4.99

ALSO BY CHRIS D'LACEY

David Rain soon discovers the dragons
when he moves in with Liz and Lucy. The pottery
Rain models fill up every spare space in the house!

But only when David is given his own special
dragon does he begin to unlock their mysterious
secrets – and to discover the fire within.

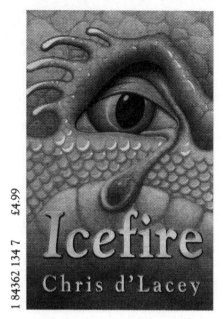

1 84362 134 7   £4.99

CHRIS D'LACEY

When David Rain is set an essay on dragons, there's
only one thing he knows for sure – he wants to
win the prize of a research trip to the Arctic.
As David begins to dig deeper into the past,
he finds himself drawn down a path from which
there is no going back...to the very heart of the
legend of dragons, and the mysterious,
ancient, secret of the icefire...

1 84121 539 2   £4.99

CHRIS D'LACEY

Jason's Aunt Hester is a grouchy old stick.
But a witch? Surely not? But then, why is there
a whole crew of pirates held prisoner in her cellar...?
Aided by Scuttle, the saltiest, smelliest seadog ever,
Jason sets out to solve the mystery and defeat
the evil Skegglewitch.

'Tis a most riotous, rib-tickling romp of a read.'
Buccaneering World

'I be laughing so much I be a-toppling overboard.'
Pirate Times

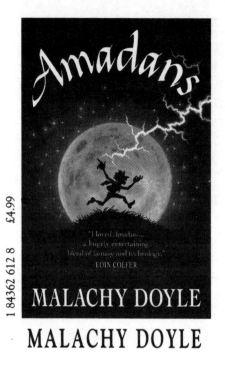

'I loved *Amadans*...
a hugely entertaining
blend of fantasy and technology.'
EOIN COLFER

MALACHY DOYLE

MALACHY DOYLE

'I've had enough of these Amadans, trying to scare
everyone,' said Jimmy. 'I think it's about time we found
out who they are and what they're up to.'

Enter the fantastical world of the Amadans in this
enthralling read.

*'I loved Amadans...a hugely entertaining
blend of fantasy and technology.'*
Eoin Colfer

£4.99

1 84121 456 6

MICHAEL LAWRENCE

Something's after Jiggy McCue! Something big
and angry and invisible. Something which
hisses and flaps and stabs his bum and generally
tries to make his life a misery.
Where did it come from?

Shortlisted for the Blue Peter Book Award

'*Hilarious.*'
Times Educational Supplement

'*Wacky and streetwise.*'
The Bookseller

ORCHARD RED APPLES

❑ *The Fire Within*	Chris d'Lacey	1 84121 533 3
❑ *Icefire*	Chris d'Lacey	1 84362 134 7
❑ *The Salt Pirates of Skegness*	Chris d'Lacey	1 84121 539 2
❑ *Amadans*	Malachy Doyle	1 84362 612 8
❑ *The Truth Cookie*	Fiona Dunbar	1 84362 549 0
❑ *Nudie Dudie*	Michael Lawrence	1 84362 647 0
❑ *The Poltergoose*	Michael Lawrence	1 86039 836 7
❑ *Do Not Read This Book*	Pat Moon	1 84121 435 3
❑ *Do Not Read Any Further*	Pat Moon	1 84121 456 6
❑ *Tower-block Pony*	Alison Prince	1 84362 648 9
❑ *When Mum Threw Out The Telly*	Emily Smith	1 84121 810 3

All priced at £4.99

Orchard Red Apples are available from all good bookshops, or can be ordered direct
from the publisher: Orchard Books, PO BOX 29, Douglas IM99 1BQ
Credit card orders please telephone 01624 836000
or fax 01624 837033 or visit our Internet site: www.wattspub.co.uk
or e-mail: bookshop@enterprise.net for details.

To order please quote title, author and ISBN and your full name and address.
Cheques and postal orders should be made payable to 'Bookpost plc.'
Postage and packing is FREE within the UK
(overseas customers should add £1.00 per book).

Prices and availability are subject to change.